FIRING SQUAD

FIRING SQUAD

Rick Roberts

WestBow
PRESS
A DIVISION OF THOMAS NELSON

WestBow Press books may be ordered through booksellers or by contacting:

WestBow Press
A Division of Thomas Nelson
1663 Liberty Drive
Bloomington, IN 47403
www.westbowpress.com
1-(866) 928-1240

ISBN: 978-1-4497-6548-4 (sc)
ISBN: 978-1-4497-6849-2 (e)

Library of Congress Control Number: 2012915765

Printed in the United States of America

WestBow Press rev. date: 9/25/2012

For my Lord, Jesus,
who gave His all for me
that I might give my all
for Him.

ACKNOWLEDGMENTS:

I want to thank best friend, Patti, who also happens to be my wife of 38 years. She endured the hours of my preoccupation with this project and proof-read everything for me and offered helpful insights.

I also want to thank my son, Joel, who squeezed the time out of his busy schedule to do the cover art for the book. I am amazed at his artistic insight.

Finally, I want to thank my daughter, Hannah, for her excitement and encouragement when she found out I was planning to publish this story.

PROLOGUE

He leaned against the post with a mixture of relief and disappointment; excitement and fear. Relief, because the moment had finally arrived. Disappointment, because it fell short of his expectations. But then, reality seldom measures up to a person's illusions. Naturally, a man would fear death; the unknown factors. How can a man know in reality what death holds?

What will it feel like? How long will I suffer before the nothingness of death swallows me?

But what excited him, what he so desired, was the relief he hoped to find in death. Justice would be served. But more importantly, he would be free of this guilt. It would all be over.

The guard approached holding a drab piece of cloth.

"No! No blindfold. And please don't tie me to the post. I'm not going anywhere. I want this."

The guard looked to his superior who, after a moment's hesitation, nodded the okay.

Twenty yards away five skilled marksmen nervously awaited the order to execute judgment.

A shudder ran the length of his body. Fear? Anticipation? Both! This was the fate he had chosen. This is what he had requested.

His knees grew weak; his breath became shallow; his mouth went dry; his chin began to tremble.

Let's end this! Get it over with!

Finally the countdown came.

"Ready!"

Here it comes.

He held his breath.

"Aim!"

I can't wait to be free.

"Fire!"

BANG!

Huh? No! This can't be happening!

CHAPTER 1

"Hey, watch me", Ben chirped. He spread his arms like a tightrope walker and wobbled across the railing. He and his cousins, Randy and Steven, were playing on their grandfather's boat trailer in the back yard. They were taking turns walking the circumference of the trailer, balancing on the rails.

"Look at me. I'm a famous acroba— Whoa!" Ben's foot slipped. He tumbled from the rail, arms and legs flailing wildly. He landed stomach first on the big round part in the middle of the axle. He didn't know what it was called, but he remembered how it felt. All of the air was pushed out of his lungs. He tried to draw in some air, but it wouldn't come. He panicked! He was sure he was dying. He turned terrified eyes to his cousins, who stood motionless, staring at him. He tried again to take a breath. After a few desperate tries, with his cousins still gawking, he finally got a squeak of air. Then, after a labored moment, another. Slowly, with strained effort, another came. The squeaks were growing longer - like the sound of air screaming from a balloon when his dad would blow it up and pinch the valve and slowly let the air out. He looked up pleadingly to find his cousins doubled over and laughing hysterically.

"Listen to Benny making those funny noises!" Randy giggled. "Haw! Haw! How do you do that, Benny?" Steven tried to imitate the sound, and they laughed even harder.

Finally, after fifteen minutes of effort, though it seemed much, much longer, Ben managed to get his breath. His cousins had run off, Ben assumed, to show their friends their imitation of Benny's squeaking sound. Ben limped to grandmamma's house. Grandmamma always made him feel better.

A sharp pain and another wheezing sound forced Ben back to the present, and the childhood memory faded. The pounding of his feet and wheezing of his lungs were the only sounds he could hear. But fear drove him forward.

"Ohhh!" His sides were cramping — no, they were tearing, he thought. "Oh. I'm dying." The world was turning dark. He fell to his knees. His forearms crashed into the ground. Twigs and dirt drove into his elbows, but he barely noticed. He had to get air into his lungs.

"Can't breathe!" Gasp! "Ohhh, I can't breathe. Gotta stop. Gotta rest. Gotta hide." He had been running for what seemed like days. Actually, it was only three hours, but his aching muscles said much longer. He had run as fast as he could for as long as he could, but he felt like he was running through quicksand. The urgency of his predicament called for speed, and lots of it.

Running was not exactly his favorite pastime. He had joined the track team back in high school, but he didn't stay with it. Running seemed like a pointless activity, particularly the long distance running. Now, he wished he had stuck with it, if for no other reason, to prepare him for this day.

His heart was thumping so hard he could see it beating through his shirt. Boom-ba. Boom-ba. Boom-ba. Boom! His lungs felt like the air had been vacuumed from them. Each gasp strained through his windpipe with a labored wheezing sound. Every breath brought another shocking, stabbing pain. His chest felt like it was pressed in a tight band. Squeezing! Crushing! He thought he might die - suffocate.

He felt like throwing up. Then, he did. A couple of times. He was hoping, just hoping that he was far enough away from his pursuers. For a fleeting moment, he didn't care. He just needed to get a few deep breaths. But the deeper he breathed, the worse it hurt.

Breathe slowly. Easy. Just keep your head.

Gradually, after what seemed an eternity of gasping for air like a goldfish on the floor, his world started to come back into focus. His labored breathing began to take on a somewhat normal pace, but he had no time to enjoy it. He had to move on.

He was in the middle of a corn field. The corn wasn't high. It was still early in the season. But if he kept low and didn't move the stalks, he might make it to the edge of the endless fields of yellow gold and find a place to hide in the woods. Several times he stopped momentarily and peeked above the growth to see if anyone was following. He hadn't seen anyone, hadn't heard anything, but he knew they probably wouldn't be far behind.

As he lay still on the ground gasping and wheezing, he tried to listen over the noises of his own body. He could barely hear anything but the pounding of the blood pulsing through his bulging veins.

God, how long have I been running? How far have I gotten? I wonder if anyone has discovered her body yet? Maybe she didn't die. Oh God, I hope she didn't die. But she sure looked dead. I wonder how far they are behind me.

He didn't know, but he sure couldn't wait around to find out. He had to quickly put as much distance as possible between himself and Murrells Inlet – and never go back.

"Oh, no!" Ben gasped. Off in the distance he heard voices. Were they looking for him? Was it the police or some vigilante mob formed in a frenzy to catch this killer? Or was it just some farmers checking their fields? He didn't really want to know. He just wanted to be away from here. He began to crawl, staying as low to the ground as he could. Several times he was tempted to take a peek, especially when there was a change in the voices. Were they getting closer? Were they getting farther away? Were they far away and yelling, or were they close and talking softly? The suspense was driving him crazy. The pain in his lungs was still severe. His legs were on fire, cramping up with charlie horses. He couldn't get up and run now if his life depended on it. And it probably did!

He crawled back and forth. Up one row a few feet, then across another a few feet. Sometimes he doubled back and changed direction, depending on where the voices seemed to be coming from. He bumped a stalk and it shook.

"Over there," someone shouted, "across the field on the left. I saw something move."

The silent fugitive panicked. He jumped up, crouching as much as he could and still run. Lucky for him, the charlie horses had released the muscles in his legs. He dashed through the higher stalks, hitting every one, leaving a swishing, rocking trail behind him. "Thump. Thud." Ears of corn were giving him quite a beating. The thought came to him that he would never eat corn again without a justified sense of revenge for the thrashing he was taking from the appendages of these unwitting assailants. But the thoughts of getting caught kept him running in spite of the agony of the whipping he was enduring. He ran with all his might, holding his sides and trying not to stir up any more fuss than was absolutely unavoidable.

He could hear feet pounding across the field – coming through the corn stalks. They couldn't see him yet, but they sure could see where he had been. Cornstalks were swaying in his wake. He couldn't tell how many pursuers there were or who they were. He didn't have time to look back to see, or even to guess how far back they might be.

"Thump. Thud." *Where did those ears come from?* His nose felt like it broke on that last hit. Blood ran down his face. He wiped it on his sleeve. Some of the blood rubbed onto a corn stalk.

Bam! *Wha...?* Bam! Bam!

Gunshots.

Oh no! It's worse than I thought. They've got guns. They don't want to catch me. They want to kill me.

Ben threw himself on the ground, bounced off several cornstalks, bruising his ribs, and he ended up face down in the dirt. "Ughh," he groaned as he rubbed his sides and tried to catch his breath. Dirt filled his mouth, nose and eyes. He shook his head and sputtered, spitting dirt and wiping his eyes.

"I think I might have hit him," a young voice called out. Sounded like a boy – maybe a teen or younger.

Another answered. "No, I don't think you're shooting in the right direction. I think he went that way."

Ben couldn't tell which direction they were talking about, but he sure hoped it was the other way. He decided to wait it out and analyze the situation. He crawled into the thickest area he could find where he could hide under the leaves of the cornstalks. He slowed his breathing and stayed as still as possible. Soon, he heard footsteps approaching. He closed his eyes and hoped that he was hidden well enough to not be detected.

Someone walked within four feet of him.

Please, don't come in this direction. Don't look over here.

He ventured a peek without moving a muscle. He just cracked open one eye and rolled it around. Through the stalks he could see a young man, maybe seventeen. Not likely part of a search party. Maybe two guys out gunning for the prize on their own. Heard about the crime and the fugitive and decided to be heroes. That would have been a dangerous game had it been anyone but Ben Wilson they were looking for. No danger there. He wasn't a dangerous criminal. At least, not yet. He was just a fool in the wrong place at the wrong time with the wrong person and the wrong ideas.

How did I get into this mess?

He heard another set of footsteps behind him and to his right. No time to move now. And no time to relax. The first guy might have walked by, but this one could stumble right over him.

Lord, help me! Oh, that's right. I'm a criminal, a fugitive on the run. I can't pray. At least, not to any God I've ever heard of. He wouldn't like what I've done.

The second boy looked to be about fifteen. He was standing just a few feet away, turning, trying to decide which way to search.

"See anything, Sam?"

"No, just … Hey, wait! There's some blood on this stalk. Looks like he headed that way." He was pointing off in a westward direction.

Whew! Ben was glad he had switched directions back and forth, especially after busting his nose on that ear of corn.

"What do you think it was, Sam? Where do you think he went?" the younger voice called ahead as he ran to catch up with Sam.

"I'm not sure, Jim. I think it mighta been an eight-point buck, maybe ten. He mighta gone into the woods over at the far end of the field. I lost him somewhere, but I think I wounded him. I'm a pretty good shot, ya know."

Thank God. They think I'm a deer, and they think they are hunters. And I'm glad they think they are better shots than they actually are.

Slowly and carefully he started crawling across the field with a new hope of escaping. These guys were not onto him. Maybe nobody was yet. Maybe nobody had tried to call or visit the apartment yet. Maybe they hadn't found her. Maybe they wouldn't put the two of them together. Maybe no one had even seen them together. Too many maybes. Better keep moving. The wannabe hunters were gone – probably lost on their own property. That gave him a chuckle. But only briefly.

Oh God, what have I done? How could this happen to me?

It didn't seem real. It was like a bad dream that he didn't want to think about right now – or ever. Maybe he could escape justice. He didn't really think so.

They always get caught in the movies. But, maybe. Just maybe.

Anyway, he would run and hide for as long as he could. He continued bellying his way across the corn field.

Suddenly, a sound unnerved him. Rattling!

Oh, no!

He looked up to see a rattlesnake two feet in front of him. It was coiled and looking straight at him, its evil eyes focused on him as if to say, "You think you can run? Not a chance. If the authorities don't get you, I'll mete out justice right here in this corn field. You're gonna die you lowlife."

The snake lunged. Ben rolled to his left. The snake missed and bounced off his arm. It coiled and prepared to strike again. Ben pulled back, and the snake came short.

What am I going to do? I've got to get out of here. Do I stay down and face the snake or jump and run and bring on the hunters?

As the rattler prepared for another attack, Ben jumped to his feet and tried to move away. The snake lunged and was blocked by a cornstalk. Then he heard the voices again.

"Hey, look. There's something over there. That's not a deer. It's a —"

The voices faded from his hearing as Ben panicked. In one unthinking, dangerously bold and profoundly foolhardy act, he reached down and grabbed the snake and threw it with all his might. It landed right between the two boys.

"What in the — Snake!" the younger boy shrieked. "It's raining rattlesnakes!"

Their rifles went airborne. The boys bolted across the cornfield leaving a trail of broken cornstalks in their path. They didn't look back. They ran to the edge of the field and back to the dirt road where Sam, the older of the two, had left his motorcycle. They ran right past the motorcycle without slowing down. They continued to the end of the dirt road, onto the highway, and headed for town.

Ben had bolted the other direction. Had he had time to think about it, he would have laughed at the thought of the two boys tearing through the community screaming about rattlesnakes falling from the sky.

The sky is falling! The sky is falling!

But they would surely report that they had seen a man in the field, and by now they might know about the girl. He had to keep running.

He soon reached the swampy forest and continued in his flight as leaves and limbs gave him another thrashing. Deeper and deeper into the woods he ran. To where, he didn't know. He just had to stay on the move.

CHAPTER 2

Ben pressed on, slower than at first, deeper and deeper into the forest. He had no idea where he was or where he was going. He just knew that he had to get as far away as possible. Whether he was traveling north or south or east or west, he didn't know. Neither did he care. He had no destination except far away, no goal except escape, no purpose except survival. Deep down, he knew that ultimately he would be caught. Eventually he would pay for his crime. But rational thinking was not an option right now. Logic was not part of the plan. There was no plan! He just had to run and run and run.

Wait! That rock! He had seen it before. And that tree! Hours ago. "Oh no! I'm going in circles." At this rate, he would be caught before the sun went down. Did they know yet?

I've got to run a straight line here. Got to find some landmark, something to guide me.

The sun was peeking through the trees.

It's late afternoon. The sun is straight in front me. I'm heading west. Okay. Keep heading toward the sun. Run!

He ran for another hour, keeping the sun directly ahead, trying to stay on course. He was still taking a beating from bushes and small trees, even occasionally running into a tree when his vision didn't match his speed.

As he ran under some thick brush, his foot caught under a log and he lunged forward, landing face first in the soft, moist ground. Dazed, he lifted himself up on his arms and attempted to get to his feet when he felt something brush against his leg. Whomp! *What was that?* He turned his face to the right only to look into a deep white throat lined with sharp dingy teeth. Whomp! He jerked his arm away just in time to avoid the gator's bite. He rolled to his left, jumped to his feet, and ran - in the wrong direction. As soon as he felt he was far enough from danger, he adjusted his course and headed back west.

Satisfied that he was, to some degree, out of danger, he breathed a sigh of relief. "I wonder how many more of those are lurking out here?" he whispered to himself. "I'd better keep my head down and my eyes to the ground."

Just then he walked between two trees and felt a massive spider web wrap around his head and arms. He thought he felt something moving in his hair. Flailing his arms desperately, he beat his head and shoulders furiously. He fell to the ground and rolled, and then thought of the possibility that he might throw himself into another alligator, or maybe a water moccasin. "God, get me out of here", he screamed. Maybe jail would be better, at least safer. He was risking his life in the swamp.

He ran quite a distance and finally stopped to rest. He sat on a felled tree, first checking thoroughly for gators, snakes, and spiders before settling down. Some time passed. How long he didn't know. It was getting dark. He had to find a place to hide for the night. Or maybe it would be better to travel at night under the cover of darkness, but with all the dangerous critters lurking out there, he wasn't sure that was the best course of action. Unable to decide, he just kept moving.

CHAPTER 3

"What have you got?" Detective George Jones asked the officer at the scene. Most people just called him 'Jonesy', though behind his back some called him 'Country', because he had the same name as the famous country singer.

Officer Cal Simmons had arrived at the Oakmoss Apartment Complex just a little after six PM responding to a call concerning the tenant in apartment G-5, Liz Fairfax. A friend, Bridget Benson, better known as 'Bebe', had tried for hours to call Liz on the phone. Finally, Bebe went to the apartment and beat on the door until she thought she heard the phone beeping inside. She suspected something was wrong and called the police.

"We couldn't get a response, so we had the manager open the apartment. We found the girl on the floor in a pool of blood, head smashed in with a bookend," Officer Simmons said.

"Motive?" Jones asked.

"Not sure. Wasn't very sophisticated. The murder weapon was laying beside the body. Nothing seems to be missing. Nothing else in the apartment was disturbed. Looks like somebody either had a grudge or just lost their cool and hit her," Simmons explained. "Doesn't look like they were trying to cover their tracks. I'm guessing we'll find fingerprints all over the murder weapon and anything else they may have handled. If they're in the system, we'll track 'em down. Open and shut."

"Yeah. Open and shut," Jones said. "I wish it was really that easy."

Come on, Jonesy. Don't be so negative, Simmons thought to himself.

"Any witnesses? Anybody see anything?"

"Nobody has come forward yet," Simmons said. "We're still knocking on doors, but so far nobody saw or heard anything. Most of the tenants were away or at the swimming pool on the other side of the building."

"Estimated time of death?" Jones asked.

"Well, we know that Miss Benson started calling at three, so we can assume that the time of death was earlier —".

"We cannot assume anything." Jones gave him an icy look.

"I only meant —"

"We do not assume a-n-y-t-h-i-n-g!" Jones raised his voice. "This is a murder investigation. We only deal with factual evidence. Where is the Medical Examiner?"

"Right behind you, sir." The voice behind him was Sidney James, Georgetown County ME. "Just finished my evaluation. I estimate time of death at roughly 1:30 PM give or take a few minutes."

"Okay," Detective Jones called out orders to everyone within hearing range. "It is now ..." he looked at his watch, "... 7:25. The perpetrator has a six hour head start. Depending on whether he or she or they are on foot or driving, they could be anywhere from thirty to three hundred miles from here. Put out an All Points Bulletin for anyone with bloodstains on their hands or clothing, and anybody acting suspicious. We really don't know what we are looking for. Has that evidence gone to the lab yet?"

"Yes sir," Officer Simmons said. "The Crime Scene Investigation team left half an hour ago with everything they collected."

"Good! Get me some answers. Soon!" Jones said. "I don't want this trail to get cold."

The officers at the scene continued to question anyone who arrived at the apartment complex on the outskirts of Murrells Inlet, hoping to find someone who had been present between the hours of 11 AM and 3 PM and may have seen or heard any suspicious activity.

Meanwhile, other officers were combing the community in an ever widening circle. Shortly after eight o'clock a junior officer with a short, brown-haired woman in tow, approached Detective Jones.

"Sir, this is Nancy Clemmons. She works at the convenience store on the other side of Highway 17. She says she saw a man running away from the Oakmoss Apartments a little before 2 PM."

Clemmons fidgeted behind the officer.

"Why am I just hearing about this now?" Jones whispered to the cop through gritted teeth. "Didn't someone question the people in that store an hour ago?"

"Uh! Yes sir," the officer said, his voice trembling, obviously intimidated by Jones. "Mrs. Clemmons was on a dinner break and just came back to the store a few minutes ago. I noticed her arrival and approached her."

"Alright, then. Thanks officer..." he studied the man's badge,"... Etheridge. You can go." He turned to the witness and launched into a series of questions. "Now, Mrs. ... Is it Mrs. or Miss?"

"Mrs. Clemmons," she said. "My husband, Randy, and I own that little store over yonder." She pointed across the highway to a white, two-story wood frame building with a faded chewing tobacco advertisement painted on the side. "We moved here from Kentucky a few years ago and bought this store. I always wanted to live in Myrtle Beach, but we couldn't afford nothin' up there. Murrells Inlet is nice, though. Did you know some of the best seafood restaurants on the Grand Strand are here in Murrells Inlet?"

"Yes ma'am," Jones said. "I grew up in Georgetown."

"Oh, well, anyway, our sons help us run the place. Our oldest, Ronnie, ain't too good with numbers, so we don't let him run the cash register. But Jimmy, he's the smart one and he —"

"Yes ma'am," Jones broke in before she went through the whole family history. "I understand you saw something."

"Well, I ain't never been involved in no murder investigation before. I hope I don't say nothing that will cause nobody no trouble.' Clemmons said.

"Don't worry about that, ma'am. Just tell me what you saw. Try to remember every detail."

"Well, at about two o'clock - I know that it was two because the Potato Chip truck comes every Wednesday at two. Anyway, while Wayne - that's the potato chip guy - while Wayne was coming into the store, I looked up to say 'Hey, Wayne', and I saw this guy running from the direction of the apartments. He kept running kind of off to the side of the road and looking back at the apartments. Then he ran off across that field over yonder."

"Where did he go from there?"

"Well, I don't rightly know. I had to get back to my customers and Wayne, the potato chip man."

"Can you describe him?"

"The potato chip man?"

Jones smiled. "No ma'am. Please describe the man you saw running across the field."

"Oh! Right! Well, I didn't see him up close, but it looked like he was wearing some kind of uniform."

"Like a work uniform, a prison uniform, a military uniform?" Jones asked.

"It kind of looked like a policeman's uniform to me."

"Okay. How tall, what color hair, shoes, any other details? Did he run with a limp? Was he carrying a weapon?

"No, I didn't see no weapon. I mean he might of had one in his pocket, but I didn't see none."

"Height?"

"Huh?"

"About how tall?"

"Ummm! A little bit shorter than that policeman over there, and he was kind of thin."

"Hey, officer. Yeah, you. How tall are you?" Jones yelled across the street.

"Five eleven, sir," the officer said.

"Was the man you saw black or Caucasian"

"He was white."

"Hair color?" Jones asked.

"Dark, and a little straggly. I think he heeded a haircut. You know, you can tell lot about a person —"

"Thank you, ma'am." Jones clipped her short again. "I think this information will help us lot. Mrs. Clemmons, you've been a great help. If you think of anything else ... Oh, by the way, have you ever seen this person here before?

"What person?" she looked around.

Jones breathed heavily trying to control himself, "The man running in the field."

"No, I don't think so."

"So you wouldn't know him if you saw him again?"

"Well, I don't know. I might. Oh! I just remembered. His ears kind of stuck out."

"Thank you, Mrs. Clemmons. We'll call you if we need anything more."

"Okay," Detective Jones turned to his team of policemen. "We have a white male, about five feet eleven inches, thin, with dark, straggly hair, big ears, and possibly wearing some kind of uniform. Get that information out and—"

"Sir." It was Officer Simmons. "Sorry to interrupt, but you're going to want to hear this. The crime lab just called. They matched the prints to a Benjamin Wilson. He's a security guard at the Ocean Highway Mall. New hire. Been on the job for two months. The Mall Office did a background check. That's why his prints were in the system. He's squeaky clean. Never been in any trouble."

"Anybody know if he had a vehicle?" Jones asked.

"Yes. He drives an older Dodge pickup truck. Mall Security just informed us that the truck is still there in the parking lot."

"Okay," Jones said. "So, unless he stole a car, he's probably still on foot. Find out if any cars have been reported missing in the vicinity of the crime. And get me all the information you can on this guy. I want to know where he's from, if he has any family in the area, who his friends are, where he hangs out, what his routines are - everything."

"I've already sent someone over for his file at the mall security office, boss," said a voice behind Jones. The detective recognized the voice without looking. It was Sergeant John Ross, from his squad.

"Ross, glad you could make it. This crime scene is getting cold," Jones said. Jones typically barked at his teammates, but nobody really took him seriously, or at least not offensively. He just liked order and swiftness. He couldn't sit still until a case was solved.

"Sorry boss, we had a real mess over at —"

"Ah save it, Johnny. I don't want excuses. I want action. Let's get the lead out, how 'bout it?" Jones said.

"Hey, lighten up, Countr...uh, Jonesy."

"I'll lighten up when you tighten up. And you'd better watch your mouth, son. I know what ya'll call me behind my back." Jones was trying to sound intimidating, but deep down he was a gentle giant, all bark and no bite ... well maybe a little bite ... a tough guy veneer to cast the Dirty Harry image. He thought it would make him more credible and effective as a detective.

John Ross walked away chuckling to himself.

"And Ross," Jones added, "get some canines over here and try to get a scent on this perp. And as soon as you get the file on this Wilson fellow, get some pictures circulating and put out an APB for him. Put it on TV. I want this guy brought in."

"Right away, boss."

CHAPTER 4

Night came. Good. Ben hoped the darkness would give him an advantage. The natural cover of night was aided by a clouded sky and a crescent moon. He would be less likely to be seen by anyone on the lookout for a fugitive.

Ben couldn't cut a straight path because of the scattered neighborhoods, but he kept weaving his way west by picking out a prominent star to follow. He still had no idea where he might be or where he would go.

As he wandered deeper into the swamplands, the ground was getting spongy. Huge tangles of gray moss draped the large oak trees that loomed all around giving the dark forest an eerie feel. The hanging moss seemed like dangling fingers groping at him – like the hand of judgment reaching for him. Cypress knees, those smooth blunted points protruding from the soft earth and shallow water, looked like claws reaching up through the ground from the pit to drag him into a miry torment. This swampy graveyard seemed to taunt him.*"You think you can escape the judgment of the law, boy? You can't escape me. You might run from the police, but the long arm of the forest will get you,"*

Ben wanted to run, especially when he walked into a hanging clump of moss. But in the darkness running was a greater threat than the grasp of the moss. Besides, there was no way to run in this mushy mess. His feet were sinking deeper into the marsh with each step, pulling out with a sucking sound. He had to struggle to keep his shoes from coming off. He would never make it barefoot out here. He had to step cautiously. He was still fearful of the gators and snakes. And the mosquitoes were feasting on him. What a miserable place! Again he entertained the thought that jail would be better, but…

Just then he heard a sound.

"Whoooo!"

"What?" Ben jerked as if he had been stabbed.

"Whooo. Whooo." His imagination was fueled by his fear. He quickly realized it was just an owl, but the sound was eerie as it carried through the swampy environs.

Getting a little jumpy, aren't we Ben?

He trudged on through the forest, the moon peeking through every so often but not nearly enough to suit him. He was basically walking blind. The water was getting deeper with each step. The swamp seemed to be growing around him.

To distract himself from fear, he began to fantasize that he was one of Francis Marion's men, the Revolutionary war hero who had lurked in these same swamps ambushing the British forces who ventured into the forest searching for freedom fighters. They called Marion 'the Swamp Fox'. Ben pictured himself darting from tree to stump, hiding behind cypress knees, picking off British soldiers with pinpoint accuracy. Every wall of moss veiled another militia-man positioned to bushwhack the unsuspecting British soldiers. Behind every cypress knee was a rebel musket primed for the red and white uniform of the enemy. In the distance he could see his commander, Francis Marion himself, riding through the swampy forest on a black steed, encouraging his men. Ben hoped Marion might come his way. What a privilege it would be to meet the great commander.

Suddenly the British had him surrounded. The trees had grown faces, donned uniforms, and produced weapons. They had him in their sights. "Ready! Aim! Fire!" As they prepared to waste him, he reached down and grabbed a snake slithering by. He tossed the snake into the midst of the soldiers. In their panic, several shot into the air, while others shot each other. Ben, the adventurous hero, grabbed a hanging vine and swung off into the brush. He let go of the vine, did a dramatic backflip into the air, and landed in the center of — Splash!

Ben gasped as he returned to reality. He had stepped into a deep spot in the swamp water and plunged face forward into the slimy soup. He came up choking. Wiping the wet mud from his face, he looked around embarrassed, as if someone might have witnessed his clumsiness.

He located the star through the thick trees and got his bearing and continued to move. Gone was the vision of history - the militia, the soldiers, the commander. Back was the reality of his dire predicament. On through the forest he pushed, hoping for a place to hide - a place to rest.

CHAPTER 5

"**D**etective Jones, we just received a report you'll be interested in. Two boys were out hunting over near Burgess and saw someone running through a cornfield. They claim he threw a snake at them. Of course, that was after they had taken a shot at him thinking he was a deer," Officer Simmons reported.

"Stupid kids! Oughta be more careful before they pull the trigger. They could have killed somebody," Jones said.

"Yeah, they probably made up that ridiculous story about the snake to draw attention away from their carelessness."

"Okay," Jones said. "As soon as you get those dogs ready get them over to Burgess and see if they can pick up a scent."

"You got it, Sir."

"Miss Benson, how long have you known the victim, Liz Fairfax?" Detective Jones asked. They were in the interrogation room at the Murrells Inlet Police Substation.

"About two years," Bebe said. "She moved here from Ohio and joined the staff at the Real Estate office where we both work ... uh, worked."

"Were you very close?

"Oh, yes. We worked together and went out for drinks several times a week after work. We had a lot in common and confided in each other. We have grown pretty close over the last two years."

"Do you know of anyone who would have reason to kill her? Has anyone, to your knowledge, threatened Miss Fairfax?"

"No! I can't imagine why anyone would hurt her. She was a nice person."

"How about boyfriends? Was she seeing anyone?" Jones continued.

"Well, I don't think she was seeing anyone seriously. She was pretty popular with the guys, though. Seems like she was with someone new every time I saw her out. She never talked about anyone special, though. I don't think she had any deep relationships with men. I always thought that was strange."

"How so?" Jones wrinkled his brow.

"Well, she was so beautiful and outgoing. You would think some guy would have swooped her up. But guys seemed to never go out with her more than once," Benson said.

"Why do you think that was?" Jones leaned forward.

"I'm not sure. I don't think she really liked any of the guys she went out with. Maybe her standards were too high. She always talked about what losers they were. I think she must have had bad taste in men. I mean, she could have had any guy she wanted. But she kept going out with guys that she couldn't stand after the first date. I guess she was just too particular."

"Did she chat with anyone on the internet – Facebook, Myspace, chat rooms, anything like that?"

"Oh my,... I don't know," Bebe said. "Do you think she made contact with some kind of sexual predator online?"

"We have to consider every possibility. Did you know of her to engage in anything like that ... computer generated relationships, I mean?"

"I honestly don't know. We never talked about it. And I never went on Facebook or any of those things. We didn't even email each other. I work with computers all day long, so when I get off work, I don't even want to see a computer. But Liz may have used it. Like I said, we didn't talk about that. It just never came up, because it wasn't something I was interested in."

"Okay, thanks. We'll be checking her personal computer and the one at work to see if we can track down anything suspicious. Our people are going through her files now," Jones said. He pressed on. "What about her parents? Do you know them?"

"She didn't talk a lot about them. I figured there might have been some tension, by, you know, just little things she said…and things that she didn't say. Her parents live in a little town outside of Cincinnati, Ohio – Bethel, I believe it was. Liz grew up there and went to the University of Cincinnati. She talked a lot about college, though."

"Oh?" Jones raised his eyebrows. "Just what did she say about college? Any problems there?"

"Well, she didn't talk much about her studies, if that's what you mean. She talked about the boys and the parties. Liz loved to party. And she loved attention from the guys. She could be quite the flirt."

"Hmmm!" He dragged that out as he let his mind work. "Back to her parents. Did you ever meet them?"

"I never met her dad," Bebe said. "She talked to her mom maybe a couple of times a month, sometimes more. She's only been back home once since she moved to Murrells Inlet, but she didn't stay long. Her mom visited once last year. I didn't get to meet her, though."

"Any siblings?

"She never mentioned any. I assumed she was an only child."

"When was the last time you saw her?" Jones asked.

"Yesterday, when we left work. I think she had a date last night."

"Have you spoken to her since then?

Benson answered quickly, "Yes, I spoke with her this morning on the phone. She was going to the mall to pick up a few items. We were going to meet afterward, I assumed around 2 PM. We get together most Saturdays about that time and go out for coffee. When I didn't hear from her, I tried to call beginning at three o'clock. By four I was getting impatient. I came over and knocked on her door. There was no answer, but her car was in the parking lot."

"What made you think something was wrong? Couldn't she have been napping or visiting a neighbor? Isn't that a possibility?"

"Well, maybe with most people, yes. But, I've never known of Liz to nap on Saturday afternoons, and like I said, we usually go out for coffee. And Liz wasn't real close with any of the people in the complex. I mean, she didn't dislike them. She just didn't mix with them much. I was her only real close friend. We had a routine on Saturdays, so I kind of panicked when… well, not really panicked, I just got concerned when things didn't seem normal, you know. So I came to the apartment and knocked on the door. There was no answer, so I put my ear to the door to see if anyone was stirring in the apartment. That's when I heard the phone beeping off the hook. Liz has … had a real pet peeve about people leaving phones off the hook. She hated ibeeping noise. So…"

"Where do *you* live Miss Benson?"

"I live in the Meadows Apartments on the other side of Route 17, not too far from here."

"Do you live alone?

"Yes… Umm. Am I a suspect here?" Bebe asked with a mixture of fear and annoyance in her voice.

"No, ma'am. No one's a suspect yet." He didn't tell her about the young man seen fleeing the scene. He wanted to hold back until she revealed all she might know. Who knows? She might be involved.

Bebe began to cry. "How could something like this happen? Who would do such a thing?"

"Miss Benson, you have been most helpful. I am sorry for the loss of your friend, but rest assured that we will find the person who did this and bring them to justice. You can count on that. We will call you if we need any further information. Again, you have been most helpful. Thank you!"

Benson was impressed. She had not seen that sensitive side of Jones. She reasoned that he must necessarily have a sensitive side in order to care enough to solve crimes – especially murder crimes. In spite of his gruffness, she liked him.

"Thank you Detective. I know you will do your best. God bless you!"

God bless you? That sounded refreshing. When you deal with crime and its perpetrators every day, 'God bless you' is not something you hear often. *I could use more of that. A lot more. And I could sure use God's help in this job.*

CHAPTER 6

Ben pressed his way through the thick murky swamp, occasionally passing through fields of marshland, sloshing through mud and peeling his way through dense reeds. He had been traveling in the darkness for several hours, only rarely seeing lights from distant neighborhood homes and an occasional lone farm. The darkness was oppressive with the slight moon overhead hidden frequently by scattered clouds. The only thing more oppressive than the darkness was the loneliness. He really couldn't think of anyone he could turn to, especially given what he had done. He had never been any trouble to anyone, but he wasn't really close with anyone either. He was pretty much a loner. Always had been.

Since the splash in the swamp water he was moving more cautiously - more slowly. He didn't need or want another mud bath.

He was again in the thick of the woods moving along the edge of a creek. Suddenly a small cabin loomed before him. It appeared to be deserted. He eased up next to the structure and peered in through a window. There was total darkness inside - even darker than the night outside. He made his way around the cabin and found a door. It was ajar. He eased it open and crept inside. Nothing stirred. As his eyes began to adjust to the blackness he could make out the shapes of a few scattered pieces of furniture. There was a table in the center of the room with maybe a couple of chairs. Beyond that possibly a fireplace. He couldn't tell for sure. To the left was a large stuffed chair. That was all he needed to see. Since the cabin was abandoned, there should not be a problem with him taking up residence for a few hours. He desperately needed to rest.

Ben eased himself into the chair and felt the tension lift from his body. Almost immediately he drifted off to sleep.

"What you doin' here, boy?"

Ben flew out of the chair and nearly sprawled out on the floor. He managed to right himself and spun around scanning the darkness. "Who said that?" he screamed.

"I did," came a voice from a dark corner. "What you doin' in my house?"

Ben strained his eyes in the direction of the voice. He could barely make out the whites of two eyes deep in the corner of the room.

"What you doin' out here in these woods" the mysterious voice demanded.

"I'm sorry. I didn't know anybody was here. I didn't know it was your house. I got lost. I was tired. I needed somewhere to rest. I'm sorry. Please don't hurt me. I'll go," Ben pleaded.

"I ain't gonna hurt you, son. I just ain't used to people wanderin' in here." The eyes were now moving toward him.

A match lit in front of the form coming forward. Then a small kerosene lamp emitted light into the room. Ben noted that the place was more furnished than he thought. There was a bed against the back wall across from what was indeed a fireplace. A bureau was at the end of the bed, clothes partially hanging out of the nearly closed drawers. Next to the fireplace was an old china cabinet stocked with a few dishes and glasses, some canned food and dry goods. Next to that was a small kitchen table, the old type with the white porcelain top with black edging. The porcelain was chipped in a few places. On the table were a few knives and a couple of forks and spoons. The room was fairly orderly and not as dirty as one would expect for a hut in the woods.

Standing beside the lamp blowing the match out was a tall skinny man with the darkest skin Ben had ever seen. His bright eyes nearly glowed against his dark skin. He looked to be in his sixties.

"What's your name, son?" the old man asked.

"I'm Ben ... Ben Wilson," he stammered. "I'm sorry mister. I wouldn't have hurt anything. I just needed to rest. Honest. I ... I'm sorry." Ben was backing toward the door as he spoke. Maybe he could run before the man could do anything to him. He knew he could be charged with trespassing. It never occurred to him that the cabin had no telephone.

"Relax Ben. I ain't mad at you. Like I said, I don't get many vis'tors out here. I'm Isaiah."

"You live out here in the woods?"

"Yep, for a few years now. Ben, how'd you get way out here?"

"I walked."

"Well son, I coulda figured that out by myself. There ain't no roads anywhere near here. So what I'm askin' is, how did you manage to get way out here in these woods and where did you come from?"

"Oh! ... Uh! ... I was just out walking and got turned around and just kinda ... found your cabin," Ben said.

"Son, why you lyin' to me? The closest road to this place is five miles away. The closest house is six miles, and you don't live there," the old man said.

"My ... my car ... it broke down, and I was —" Ben started, but Isaiah quickly cut him off.

"Please, don't keep makin' up stories, Ben. If you was on the road you wouldn't have walked into the woods to find help. Boy, you runnin' from somethin'? You in some kinda trouble?"

Dejectedly, Ben dropped his chin to his chest and sighed, "Yeah. I ... I hurt somebody."

"Hmmm," Isaiah said. "I thought so. You look real troubled. And real tired. Why don't you lay down and get some sleep. We'll talk later.

But first, let's get you out of those wet clothes. What kind of uniform is that?"

"Security guard. I work at the Ocean Highway Mall in Murrells Inlet. You know about malls?"

Isaiah grinned. "Yeah. I know about malls. I ain't been out here in the woods all my life." He chuckled as he searched through a drawer.

He gave Ben a pair of jeans that almost fit and a denim shirt. Then he directed Ben over to the small bed. Ben protested, but the old man insisted. Isaiah sat back in the padded chair and soon both men were sound asleep.

CHAPTER 7

"I didn't shoot that guy! I swear! I didn't shoot him," Sam yelled hysterically as he was escorted into the interrogation room at the Murrells Inlet Police Sub-station. "Please don't put me in jail! It was an accident! We thought he was a deer!" he continued to scream.

"Hold on son," Detective Jones tried to calm him. "Nobody wants to put you in jail. We just want to find out what happened. Now, just start from the beginning."

"Okay," the teen said excitedly, only slightly less hysterical than before. "I was born in Myrtle Beach, and then we moved to Pawley's Island, and—"

Jones almost laughed but sternly interrupted. "I don't mean that beginning. Let's just start from where you boys went hunting. Start from the time you arrived at the scene of the incident."

"Incident! What incident?... Oh! You mean when we shot the guy ... I mean ... No! I didn't mean to say we shot him. We didn't shoot the —"

"Just tell me about your hunting trip, Sam." Jones persisted.

"Oh! ... Well, Jim and I decided to go hunting, so we took my motorcycle and rode over to the cornfield off of Waterhall Drive out near the golf course. We were walking through the cornfield, like we always do, to get to the woods. We always hunt there. We got permission, honest!"

"It's okay, son," Jones assured him. "You're not in trouble. Just tell me the story." *This kid is gonna drive me over the edge.*

"Okay. So me and Jim, we're going across the cornfield when we see this deer, at least we thought it was a deer."

"What exactly did you see?" the detective pressed in. "Did you see a deer, or did you see a man, or what exactly did you see?"

"Umm! We saw the cornstalks shaking and something moving through them. I figured it was a deer and took a shot. There's never anybody out there. We never thought about it being a person," Sam said.

"When did you realize it was a man? Did you actually see him?"

"Well ... we were walking through the cornstalks looking for the deer, or what we thought was the deer. We were going back and forth trying to find it when, all of a sudden, this guy jumps up and starts running across the field. About the time we saw him, this snake comes falling from the sky and almost landed on us. We dropped our guns and ran."

"Can you describe him?"

"Oh, it was about maybe four feet long and —"

"Sam," Jones stopped him, "we're not really interested in the snake ..." he sighed "... unless it bit you. Did the snake bite you, Sam?"

"No, sir."

"Then, Sam, I ... don't ... really ... care ... what ... the snake ... looked ... like." Jones was losing the battle to control his patience. "I ... don't ... know ... if ... you ... are ... playing ... with me ... or ... just ... frightened. I ... just ... want ... you ... to ... con-cen-trate ... and tell me, ... can you ... describe ... the ... man, ... the ... man ... in ... the ... cornfield?"

"Oh! ... Uh! ... Not really," Sam said. "We didn't hang around after the snake dropped out of the sky."

"Think Sam. Can you remember anything?"

Sam closed his eyes and wrinkled up his face like he was trying to see it again in his mind. "Uh! Yeah!" He opened his eyes and looked at the officer standing guard by the door. "I think he was dressed in blue, like a police uniform."

"Hmm! That makes sense!" Jones muttered.

"Why does that make sense?"

Jones ignored the question. "Did you notice which way he went?"

"I don't know, sir. He ran toward the woods, but there's woods on three sides of that field, so I didn't notice which direction."

"Okay, thanks Sam. I appreciate your cooperation." Jones gathered his notes and stood.

"Umm! There's something else, sir."

"What's that, son?"

"I think I might have wounded him."

Jones put his notes back on the table, sat back down, and leaned toward the boy. "Why do you think that?"

"We saw some blood on a cornstalk. That's why we were searching the field. I was hoping we'd find a dead buck."

Jones dismissed Sam and interviewed Jim. He got basically the same story with the exception that Jim kept insisting that he never fired his gun.

"It was Sam! He shot the guy. I didn't do anything. You can check my shotgun."

"We did," Jones said. He glared the little traitor with disgust.

⤳

"Mr. and Mrs. Fairfax," Detective Jones said with all the sensitivity he could muster, "I'm Detective George Jones. Thank you for taking this time to talk with me. I know this is a tragic time for you. Do you mind if I ask you a few questions about your daughter?"

The Fairfaxes had caught the first flight out of Cincinnati as soon as they got the call on Saturday afternoon. They flew into Charleston, rented a car, and drove two and a half hours north on Route 17 to Murrells Inlet.

"Anything we can do to help catch her killer, detective," said Martha Fairfax through tears. "I can't believe my baby is gone."

"I'm so sorry for your loss, ma'am. What can you tell us about her?" Jones looked from Mrs. Fairfax to Mr. Fairfax and back a couple of times trying to read them.

Mrs. Fairfax was truly broken up - an emotional wreck distraught over her daughter's death. Mr. Fairfax looked unmoved, almost uncaring, but not exactly. Jones was trying to determine if the man was angry that his daughter was dead or just angry at his daughter. He didn't appear to be too upset that she was gone.

Mrs. Fairfax responded quickly, "She was a good student, very popular, and a hard worker. She had a great future ahead …" She broke down and couldn't finish her sentence.

Mr. Fairfax jumped in. "She was a tramp. I'm not surprised this happened. I've been expecting some kind of trouble from her."

Jones' mouth dropped open. Not that he hadn't seen hard, angry, uncaring parents before. But it always shocked him no matter how many times he witnessed such a display. Since his own daughter had died in a car accident seven years ago and his wife left him two years later, he had a deep appreciation for what he didn't have. It always bothered him when people didn't appreciate what they did have.

"Yeah, she was popular alright, but only with the boys. She flaunted her good looks and had a stream of boyfriends, most of whom I didn't approve of. I knew she was sleeping around and building herself a bad reputation, as well as ruining mine. I figured her behavior would get her into trouble."

"Oh Harvey, don't talk about her like that. For goodness sake, I know you had your fights with Elizabeth, but honey our baby is dead. Let her have some dignity," Martha said.

"Well, if she had practiced a little dignity in life, I'd be glad to show her a some dignity in death," he shot back. The man was bitter.

Jones was getting a pretty good picture of the Fairfax family background, but he also realized that both parents were in shock and their reactions had to be viewed in that light. He tried to redirect the mood with another question.

"Mr. and Mrs. Fairfax, do you know anything about her current friends or routines that would help us determine what happened and why?"

Martha answered, "No. Since Elizabeth left Ohio we haven't been able to keep up with her friendships and such. She's only been home once since she moved out, and that visit didn't go so well." She cut an icy glare at her husband.

"I understand," Jones said trying to diffuse the tension building. This was headed for disaster.

"Can you think of any reason why someone would want to take her life? Any old enemies or situations from her past that would lead to something like this?"

"No! She's never been in trouble or had any serious problems with anyone. She didn't take drugs or anything like that. She was a good person." Martha sounded like she might be trying to convince herself.

"Come on and face it, Martha," her husband barked. "She was a bad seed!"

"She was *our* bad seed, Harvey!" Martha barked back. "How can you act so ..." She was at a loss for words. "She was our baby. She was our flesh and blood. When did you stop being aware of that?"

Harvey had no comeback. He sat stone-faced, except that now his face was turning red.

Martha wasn't finished. "Don't you realize that Elizabeth was a product of what *we* made her? She lived in our home for eighteen years. We raised her. We were supposed to mold her and prepare her for life. Maybe you should stop blaming the seed and take a look at the farmer!"

After an awkward moment of silence Detective Jones and Mrs. Fairfax continued to talk, but Harvey didn't hear a word. Martha's words had thrust him into a reality he had long denied. She *was* their flesh and blood. She *was* their baby. And *now* she was gone. Now he would *never* have a chance to repair their relationship. That hadn't occurred to him until this moment. He began to slowly tremble. Tears began to swell in his eyes. Soon they were rolling down his cheeks. After a few moments, Harvey Fairfax began to quietly sob. The voices in the room stopped. They slowly turned to see Harvey break down and wail as the horror crashed in on him. No one spoke.

CHAPTER 8

Ben awoke to the smell of bacon. He slowly opened his eyes hoping that he would find himself in his own bed and that yesterday had just been a bad dream.

It wasn't.

He could hear the call of birds echoing through the forest. Pinpricks of sunlight streamed across the room like laser beams, shining through the slats of the aged wooden walls of the small cabin. He heard movement in the room - the shuffling of feet - dishes touching the surface of a table - the sound of metal gently scraping against metal.

"Mornin' Ben Wilson," Isaiah called out. "Ya' hungry?"

Ben sat up and threw his legs over the edge of the thin mattress. He looked at the older man standing at a small camping stove, one that looked really ancient. He was stirring eggs. There was a plate of bacon on the table. He detected a whiff of coffee.

"Uh! Yeah," Ben yawned. "I guess I am." He stood up and took a couple of unsteady steps. His muscles ached from all the running. His body gave every indication of the beating he had received in his flight through the cornfield - and the forest. Emotionally he felt drained. He wished that the whole incident wasn't real, but his bruised and sore body told him otherwise.

"Where am I? I mean, exactly where is this place? I got kind of turned around last night."

"Well, you're kind of in the middle of nowhere, which makes me wonder why you're here. You're in the woods about ten miles northwest of Murrells Inlet."

"Why do you live way out here?" Ben asked, not considering the fact that the man didn't owe him any explanation.

"Well Ben, that's a long story. I just ain't got much use for bein' 'round people. Me and society parted ways a long time ago," Isaiah said. He hoped Ben would leave it at that, but he didn't.

"Why? Don't you like people?"

"No! That's not it. People don't much like me."

"Why wouldn't people like you?"

"Well, people are kinda scared of me."

"What are they scared of? You don't seem scary to me."

Isaiah let out a deep sigh. There was no getting around it. "Ben," Isaiah hesitated, shook his head and finally said , "I did somethin' bad. Like I 'spect you done."

Ben blushed. "Wha—t did you do, Mr. Isaiah?"

"Just Isaiah, son," the old man said. "A long time ago, I got in a fight. I killed a man ... hit him with a beer bottle and cut his throat with the broken glass. I spent a lot of years in prison. When I got out most people steered clear of me. So, I decided to steer clear 'a them."

"Wow!" Ben's jaw dropped wide.

"I was a bad man back then, Ben. Fightin' and drinkin' all the time. In trouble a lot. I ain't like that no more. But people don't forget."

"So what made you change? Prison?"

"No. But it was somethin' that happened in prison."

"What happened?" Ben asked, his eyes as wide as saucers. "Did somebody threaten you? Did they rough you up? Did they beat you down? Did they r..." he caught himself. He couldn't go there.

"Actually, it was a preachin' service," Isaiah said.

"What? A preacher man changed you?" Ben said.

"No! It weren't the preacher man hisself. It was what he said."

"Oh! So you got religion," Ben said. A mocking snarl curled his lip.

"No! I ain't got much use for religion. I got somethin' better."

"What do you mean? I thought you said it was a preaching service."

"Yeah, it was a preachin' service. The preacher tol' me that God loved me. He said that God could forgive me for all the awful things I done," Isaiah explained. "I couldn't believe that. But I felt like he was lookin' right at me - like he was talkin' to me and nobody else."

Ben sat with arms folded across his chest.

"He said that God sent Jesus down here to earth to pay for my sins ... to pay for *my* sins, Ben." The old man was near tears. His voice was thick with emotion. "While I was sittin' there wonderin' why God would do that for me, the preacher man said that God did it because he cared about me."

Ben unfolded his arms and leaned forward slightly, hands on his knees.

"Nobody ever cared about me. I was jes' some useless ole' drunken, brawlin' troublemaker. But the preacher man said that God loves us even when we're at our worst - that Jesus died for sinners, not just for good folks. I tell you, Ben, my thinkin' said that couldn't be true - not for me - but somethin' way down inside 'a me said it was. When he gave the call, I went down there and I prayed with that preacher man, and I asked God to forgive me, and I asked Jesus to change me, and he did, Ben. I ain't never been the same."

Tears were flowing down the old man's face.

Ben just sat there enraptured by this display of emotion. He had no idea how to respond.

CHAPTER 9

It was Sunday noon, almost twenty four hours after the crime.

"Ross! Where are those dogs? The trail's getting colder by the minute!" Detective Jones was ranting. "And has anybody tracked down Wilson's parents yet?"

"Hey, take it easy, Jonesy," John Ross said.

"I'll take it easy when you make it easy," Jones shot back.

Ross grinned at his colleagues, "He lo— ves his one-liners, doesn't he?" He turned to Jones. "Okay, boss. The canine unit is outside ready to go. Wilson's parents are driving up from Georgetown right now."

"Well now, that's fine detective work, Ross. All the way down in Georgetown and it only took you fourteen hours to find them," Jones said. Georgetown was twenty five miles south on Route 17.

"Sorry, boss. They were visiting relatives last night in Andrews and didn't come home until this morning. It would have taken longer if they hadn't stopped by their house on the way to church and found the officers waiting for them. We had a squad car at their house all night."

Jones nearly exploded. "John, I don't want to hear your excuses. I just want results." He caught himself and relented. "Hey, I'm sorry. I'm just tired. It's been a long night. I know ya'll are doing your best. Just keep up the good work, and let's get this thing over with."

The room was hot and stuffy. The air conditioners had been pumping all day and the thermostat was set on sixty, but coastal South Carolina was sweltering today at one hundred and one degrees. It was mid-August and you couldn't find a cool place in an ice house freezer on a day like today. Without tree cover the flat roof was transferring heat into the building, and at nearly one 1:30 PM the sun was just reaching into windows on the west side of the building, making every room on that side heat like a convection oven.

Detective Jones, who usually dressed like a men's store manikin had his tie and top button loosened and his shirt collar slightly pulled open. Sweat was beading down his face, but mostly it was running down his neck and into his shirt. Everyone else was sweating as well. Shirts were wet and clingy, and nobody really wanted to put forth any effort at anything other than fanning themselves.

Ross said to Jones, "I really don't understand people coming to a South Carolina Resort and spending thirty minutes in a sauna working up an artificial heatstroke. Ten minutes in this in this sub-station and you're good to go. We should be charging admission."

Jones grunted in agreement as he slung a fingerfull of sweat from his brow onto the floor.

"Let's see if we can round up a couple of box fans to help in here. A hot, sweaty witness isn't going to be at his sharpest," he said to anyone who might be listening - anyone who hadn't been put to sleep or incapacitated by the heat.

"A hot, sweaty officer won't be much good either," Ross said.

Simmons had returned to duty and was helping with various aspects of the investigation. In fact, it was he who had summoned in the canine unit and given them the coordinates to work with. "I'll see what we can round up. You want the Wilsons in the interrogation room?" he asked.

"Wow, Simmons! You are psychic, aren't you?" Jones rolled his eyes as he spoke.

"Oh give me a break, Country," Simmons said. Then he froze."That just slipped out," he whispered to Ross.

Jones popped off, "I'll give you a break when you get awake! And you better watch that mouth of yours."

Ross snickered and quietly voiced to Simmons and the rest of his team, "Whew! He's on a roll today. Better watch him."

They all shared a quiet laugh. Jones pretended not to notice.

⌒

Fred and Mary Wilson were ushered in by a young officer. Fred was about five foot ten, medium build, graying brown hair, and sported a handlebar mustache - waxed and curled. He looked like something from a barber shop quartet and smelled of motor oil. Jones figured him to be a mechanic. He looked fifty-ish, as did his wife. Mary had a matronly look, not high class but modest and guarded. Her hair was dark with no signs of gray, but was probably darker than it was supposed to be.

Jones greeted them warmly, as if this were a casual visit. "Mr. and Mrs. Wilson, please have a seat. I'm Detective Jones. Thank you for coming in today. I'm so sorry to have to trouble you on a Sunday afternoon."

"Oh, just call us Fred and Mary," Mrs. Wilson smiled. Then her expression turned serious. "This thing they are saying about Ben, is it true? Did he hurt someone? He's never been violent."

"Well, ma'am, we're not certain of anything yet. There is just evidence that your son was in the apartment where we found a girl's body, and a witness saw a man matching his description fleeing the scene. We're investigating the matter and would like to bring Ben in for questioning. Would you have any idea where we can find him?"

The Wilson's looked at each other. Fred responded, "No, sir. He usually comes over for dinner on Sunday afternoons. He lives up here in Murrells

Inlet, so we don't see him much through the week. He might be at our house right now."

"Okay. We have officers at your house watching for him and officers at his apartment. He didn't go home last night. If he shows up at either location we'll see him. Are there any relatives he might go to?"

"I doubt it," Fred said. "Most of our relatives live in Alabama."

"Alright," Jones said, "We'll need addresses and phone numbers so we can check and see if he contacts anyone. It's very important that we talk with him."

"We'll be happy to provide all the information you need, detective," Mary said, "but I'm sure you're wrong about Ben. Ben has always been well mannered and very gentle. I can't imagine him hurting anyone."

"Well, ma'am, I hope you're right. There may have been an accident, or possibly Ben witnessed a crime and ran away because he was afraid. That's one reason we need to talk with him. Maybe he can clear himself and help us catch the killer."

"I'm sure that's what happened," Mary assured him.

Fred spoke. "I can't imagine Ben being in this girl's apartment unless he went there with somebody else. Ben is real shy, especially around girls. I don't think he's ever even been on a date."

"Well, that is helpful information," the detective replied.

They spent another half hour talking about Ben's habits, temperament, and background, but most of the information simply confirmed what had already been said. Ben Wilson didn't fit the profile of any killer, but many of the perpetrators of crimes didn't. The police were no closer to finding Ben, or the truth, than they were one hour ago.

CHAPTER 10

"So, if your life changed so much after you got religion, why are you living alone in the woods?" Ben asked Isaiah.

"I tol' you," Isaiah said sternly, "I didn't get no religion. Religion just seems to make people narrower and meaner, but only they think they's better. I got Jesus. I got a relationship with my Maker. I didn't get no religion."

"Okay! Okay! I'm sorry," Ben backpedaled. "If *Jesus* changed your life so much, why are you living out here all by yourself?"

"Well, you know, Ben, God forgives, but people has a hard time forgettin'. When I came back from prison, I couldn't get no job. People looked at me suspicious-like. They wouldn't talk to me. Kids would run away from me. People would cross to the other side of the street to avoid me. Even the church folk wouldn't have much to do with me. Oh, they would smile and nod nice enough at services, but they'd stay away from me otherwise."

"That's awful," Ben shook his head. "That's not fair."

"No, it ain't," Isaiah said. "But life ain't about fair, Ben. It jes' is what it is. Anyway, I jes' got tired of dealin' with it. I figured if I made people that uncomfortable, and they sure was makin' me uncomfortable, I'd just move away from 'em."

"So, you moved out here in the woods."

"Yep!"

"Did you build this cabin yourself?"

"Nope. A man I used to work for give it to me. It was an old huntin' cabin he had. He didn't come out here no more after he retired, so he give it to me outright. He even wrote it down all legal." Isaiah pointed to a letter in an old picture frame on the wall. In it was a handwritten document that read, 'I, Cyrus Morris, hereby give my cabin in the woods of Georgetown County near the town of Burgess and the half-acre of land around it to Isaiah Washington.' It was signed by Morris and an attorney and was stamped with legal embossing. There was no glass in the frame.

"Wow! That was nice," Ben said.

"Mr. Morris tried to get me a job, but he couldn't convince nobody to hire me. It's jes' as well, though. I'm better off out here by myself."

"Man, that's sad," Ben said.

Isaiah nodded. Then he leaned forward, elbows on his knees, looked Ben in the eye, and said, "So, what's your story?"

CHAPTER 11

"Okay, turn them loose," Lt. John Ross instructed the canine unit. Three dogs were released into the corn field. The dogs scampered around the field like they were running through a maze. The officers had retrieved a shirt from the floor of Ben's apartment. The dogs had been prepped and were searching for a trail.

"Boy, either these dogs can't find a scent or this guy ran all over the field," Sergeant Harry Crowe said. "I haven't seen them run this wild since they got sprayed by a skunk last year. Now that was a sight to see. Those hounds were useless for three days. Haw! Haw!" Several members of the team joined in the laughter.

Finally, after twenty minutes of gallivanting, the dogs converged on the western corner of the field at the edge of the woods. Then dogs and officers began to follow the scent into the woods. The officers found plenty of broken limbs and trampled weeds, even some fragments of cloth from a torn shirt. The material was consistent with a uniform such as that of a security guard.

"This guy sure wasn't concerned about covering his tracks," one of the officers said. "Bad for him; good for us."

Two hours into the search they came to the edge of the marsh and the dogs lost the scent. Footprints were detected at ever deepening degrees in the mud leading into the water.

"Hey, Lieutenant Ross," Crowe called into his speaker phone, "we've got footprints going into the water, but the dogs lost the scent at the edge of the marsh."

"And?" Ross said back.

"What do you want us to do?"

"Well, in the words of Detective Jones," Ross said, "Get into that swamp and pick up that trail again! Do I have to come there and hold your hand?"

"But Lieutenant!" Crowe said, "He could have gone anywhere!"

"Then I suggest *you* go everywhere."

"What?" Crowe snapped back.

Ross blew out a blast of air. "How many dogs do you have out there, Sergeant?"

"Three."

"And how many men?

"Six including me."

"Crowe, you got your snake boots on?" Ross asked.

"Do I have my snake boots on? Do I have snake my boots on, you ask! Do you your pants on, Ross? Of course, I have my snake boots on! Do you think I'm an idiot?"

"Well, the thought has crossed my mind, Harry," Ross chuckled.

"Very funny, John. Okay! I'm here at the edge of the marsh ... with my snake boots on. What are your instructions?"

"Sergeant Crowe, I suggest you divide up and go in three directions until somebody picks up a trail. You think you can handle that?" Ross said "I declare, ya'll act like a bunch of babies."

"Well John, we're not paid to think. That's your job."

"Harry, I've got half a mind to come out there and kick your butt, which is what Jones'll do to me if you don't find something soon."

"Yeah, well you're not the one out here sloshing around in the muddy swamp."

"Crowe, one more whiny word, and I'll —"

"Okay! Okay! We're going. Don't give yourself a heart attack. Man! What a grouch!"

CHAPTER 12

"Well ... ummm ... I, uhh—" Ben stammered.

"Just spit it out, boy," Isaiah said.

"Well, I ... got off my shift at the mall ... I'm a security cop there."

"Yeah, you tol' me that. Get on with it."

"Okay, I got off my shift at noon ... well, my shift really ended at eight, but I worked half of another guy's shift as a favor because he had to —"

"Son, you're gonna talk me to death 'fore you ever get to the point."

- Twenty six hours ago —

Ben clocked out at noon. He walked out of the staff room down the inner hall behind the stores, pushed the release bar and walked through a doorway that led into the main mall area.

He stopped in the food court and bought a cup of coffee. He strolled slowly through the mall, not really having anywhere in particular to go, and lost himself in a daydream.

As he walked through the mall, Ben noticed a pretty young lady with short red hair sitting on a bench in the common area. She seemed to be staring at him. He tried not to look - he was terribly shy - but unwittingly he slowed his pace and chanced a glance her way. She flashed him a broad smile.

It was then that he gave her a lingering look and noticed how gorgeous she was. Bright green eyes, long swooping lashes, a dainty nose, perfect teeth, and a very seductive smile. She wore a short white skirt exposing shapely legs crossed at the knees. Her dark blue shirt had the word "sexy" written across the front in fancy script with sparkles - and Ben agreed that she was.

"Hey, good looking!" Ben heard the words like a distant echo. He knew she wasn't talking to him. Girls never spoke to him. And he knew he wasn't anywhere in the neighborhood of good looking - probably not even in the universe of good looking. He kept walking.

"You, in the uniform." Ben slowly looked around for another uniformed person in the vicinity. There were none. He looked back in her direction. She had her head cocked in a seductive way and was staring straight at him.

"You sure look handsome in that uniform," she said.

Ben still didn't believe she was addressing him. He couldn't remember the last time he had talked with a female younger than his mother except to ask about a homework assignment in high-school, and even that hadn't gone so well. He had once worked up enough nerve to ask Brenda Schwartz, a girl he had known since fifth grade, for a date a couple of years ago during his senior year, and she laughed in his face. That forced Ben deeper into his shell, and he hadn't looked a girl in the eye since. Yet, here was this 'babe' beckoning to him. No! It was just his imagination.

I'd better get out of this mall before I embarrass myself.

"I said you look handsome in that uniform." He looked up, and she fluttered her eyes.

Ben looked at the floor and said, "It's just ... I mean, I'm just a —"

She interrupted before he could finish. "You look like a big strong soldier. Or maybe a policeman. Are you a policeman?"

"No," he stammered. "I'm ... I'm a security guard." He felt awkward. Then he blurted, "For the mall. I mean, I'm a security mall guard ... I mean a mall guard ...I mean, I - am - a - mall - security - guard," he finally managed. Ben was so nervous he still wasn't sure he got it right.

"Well, I think a man in a uniform is handsome. Why don't you sit down beside me, handsome?"

Ben thought he might fall down. He hesitated, then sat, almost missing the bench completely. He couldn't even see straight. He caught himself at the last second and righted himself on the bench.

She put her hand on his shoulder and said, "I'm Liz. What's your name?" Her hand felt hot on his shoulder - or was it just him?

"My name is Ben ... Ben Wilson."

"Well Ben Wilson, I've seen you around the mall, and I think you're hot."

The two continued with some small talk for about ten minutes, but Ben had no idea what they talked about. Between his painful shyness and his wonder at the fact that this amazing woman was even giving him the time of day had him in an other-worldly spell.

He zoned back in to hear her saying, "Would you like to come over to my place for a visit, or do you have to go back to work?

"Uh! Sure!" he managed to sputter.

"Sure you'd like to come over, or sure you have to go back to work? Which is it, soldier-boy?"

"I'm not a sol ... uh, sure, I'll come over."

Was this really happening? Ben wasn't sure. He thought he might be dreaming, and he hoped he didn't wake up. Ever! A girl actually was talking to him. A girl actually thought he, Ben Wilson - 'loser' Ben Wilson - was good looking. A girl actually invited him to her house. If only Brenda Schwartz could see him now. If only the guys could see him now. No! Better that the guys can't see him. One of them would surely steal this opportunity away from him.

He blindly followed her to the mall exit and into the parking lot.

Liz spoke to him and he heard her through the fog that was billowing through his mind, "We'll take my car, and I can bring you back here later. It's not far." She didn't give him time to answer. She took him by the hand and led him to her Chevy Cobalt. It was a nice car. He was glad he didn't have to let her see his old truck.

⤺

"Man, that girl had her clutches in you," Isaiah said. "That's when you shoulda' run the other way."

"Yeah! I wish I had. But I never had a girl treat me nice before," Ben said. "I should have known it wasn't real."

"Go on," Isaiah prodded him.

⤺

Liz drove them to the Oakmoss Apartment Complex five miles from the mall down Route 17. They got out of the car and she led him up to apartment G-5. She inserted the key, tilted her head back and grinned at Ben, turned the key and pushed open the door. Ben followed her into a spacious living room-kitchen combination. The apartment was much more upscale than his. It was newer, larger, and definitely cleaner than his.

As he entered the front door, the kitchen area was to the left. The refrigerator was beside the door. Beyond that was the kitchen sink, with a window looking out into the parking lot. The counter extended to the corner, ran along the left wall for a few feet and then extended out toward the opposite wall, forming a breakfast bar separating the kitchen from the living room.

An 'L' shaped sofa graced the far corner with a television on the opposite wall, and there was a bookshelf to the left. Doors to the bedroom and bath were on the right wall. Both were open. At the far wall were sliding glass doors leading to a tiny deck overlooking the inlet. There was a slight view of the ocean between the Palmetto trees and condominiums.

"Nice place," Ben mumbled.

Liz grabbed a couple of bottles of sparkling water from the refrigerator. "Thanks," she said. "Have a seat." She plopped down on the sofa and patted the space beside her. "Right here."

When she plopped down her skirt rode high up on her thigh exposing more than should have been. Ben noticed. Liz noticed that Ben noticed. She did nothing to correct it.

Ben sat, rather uncomfortably, beside her, leaving a few inches between them. Liz noticed. Ben noticed that Liz noticed. She scooted closer to him till their legs were pressed together. Ben wasn't sure how to react, so he did nothing.

Liz took a sip from her water bottle, leaned closer to Ben's face and asked, "So, where are you from, Ben Wilson?"

Ben's mouth was dry. He took a sip of water. "I'm ... I'm from Georgetown ... about twenty five miles south of here. My parents live in an area called Maryville. Where are you from?" He was trying to keep up his end of the conversation, though he didn't know how.

Liz said with a flourish, "Oh, I was born in France." She lied. "Yes, my father is an ambassador. My parents lived in Paris when I was born. Then we moved to Germany and Spain and ... well, we lived all over Europe."

Every time Liz told her story it got more outlandish. Nobody would be impressed with a girl from a small town in Ohio. She desperately needed to make an impression on every guy she met.

"I came back to the United States to go to college ... at Harvard. My parents live in Hong Kong now," she continued the ruse.

"Wow!" Ben said. "I don't think my parents have ever been any further away than Florida." It was working. He truly was impressed.

"Yes," Liz continued to spin her yarn, "I could have gone to one of the universities in Europe, but my parents felt that I should get to know my country of origin." She was enjoying his awed expression.

Ben was completely swept off his feet at this attention from someone of the opposite sex. He would have been impressed with anything. He thought back at all the times he had been made fun of because of his big ears, his clumsiness, and his shy, self-conscious nature. His lack of social skills was overwhelming in his present situation.

Liz moved even closer. She put her hand on the back of his neck and leaned in. Her breath was hot on his cheek.

"Ben, I think you're sexy. Do you think I'm sexy?" she whispered close to his ear while she twirled the hair on his temple with her finger.

His heart fluttered. He tried to speak, but nothing would come. He cleared his throat and croaked, "Uh! Yeah! I think you're ... real sexy." He barely got the words out audibly.

"Do you want to kiss me?"

Before he could answer she touched her lips to his. Ben was about to suffocate. It dawned on him that this was his first kiss. Twenty two years old and he'd never worked up the nerve to kiss a girl.

"Ben," she breathed, "do you have a girlfriend?"

"No," he managed to squeeze the word out.

"Have you ever ... been with a girl?" She sensed his innocence.

"What ... what do you mean?"

"You know," she teased, "been with a girl ... in an intimate way."

He didn't want to admit his innocence with this worldly-wise woman. Again, before he could form an answer, she pressed her lips against his, hard and passionate. He couldn't breathe. He had dreamed about, but never really anticipated, what this would feel like. She hung on for what seemed an eternity, passionately kissing his lips, stroking his neck.

Ben felt his face flushing. His chest was pounding. His pulse was racing.

Liz pressed against him tightly. He could feel her body against his arm. "You want me, don't you Ben?" she panted in his ear.

Ben reached down and hesitantly touched her knee. His head was spinning. His hand was trembling. She seemed to encourage it. He laid his hand on her leg just above her knee and began to gently stroke it. She was furiously kissing him. He slowly moved his hand up her thigh until he touched the hem of her skirt.

Smack! Ben's cheek was suddenly stinging like fire. "What ... what happened?" The room momentarily went black. When he regained focus he was glaring at a raging Liz.

"How dare you!" she screamed.

"But ... but, I thought —"

"You thought what? You thought a loser freak like you was going to make it with a girl like me! Yeah. Right. You deluded pervert."

"But you —".

"I what? I invited you over. I felt sorry for you with your big ears and your stupid hair and that goofiness you call a personality."

"I don't understand. You kissed me. You told me I was sexy."

What was it with this girl? Was she some kind of sadistic psycho? A minute ago she was crawling all over him. Now she was treating him like a rapist.

"Do you think anybody would believe that, you ugly sicko! I should call the police. You can't come in here and molest me like that!" Liz was yelling at the top of her lungs.

Ben worried someone might hear her and call the police.

"Please calm down," he cried. "I didn't do anything wrong."

"Sure you did do something wrong. You dared to even entertain the thought that *I* would have anything to do with *you*." She started screaming again. "You're a freak ... a pervert ... a loser! Loser! Loser!"

"Please stop. Don't yell at me. Don't call me those things." Ben cried.

"You disgusting fool. You pathetic slime," she continued to spit the words at him. "Ha! Ha! Ha! Ha! Lo...s...er! *Me* ... with ... *you*? I think I would throw up. Hah! Ha! Ha! Ha!" It was a wicked, evil, hideous laugh.

The humiliation was unbearable. Ben was hyperventilating. The world was spinning out of control. What kind of game was this?

It was Liz's game. She played it well, and she played it often. She would lure guys in, seduce them but only let them get so far, and then humiliate them.

Ben couldn't take any more.

"Freak! Retard! Stupid! Loser!" She shrieked.

"Stop! Stop!" Ben was holding his head, covering his ears. Tears were streaming down his cheeks.

"Oh! And now he's a cry-baby, too. The big, tough soldier-boy in the uniform is a loser cry-baby." Her onslaught was relentless. "I think the poor baby needs his mommy," she mocked in a sing-song voice.

Ben screamed. Everything was going dark. His face felt hot. His mind was reeling.

"Loser! You pervert loser! You ugly, stupid, cry-baby loser!"

"Stop! Stop!" Blind rage engulfed him. His whole body began to tremble.

"You idiot! You dumb, stupid idiot!" She got louder. She was in his face. "Loser! You pathetic los—"

Suddenly her words stopped. Ben stood there in a blind fog wondering why the room had gone deafeningly silent. Was he unconscious? Had it all really been a nightmare?

He blinked his eyes and saw why. Liz was lying on the floor. The side of her head was caved in. Blood was oozing from her cracked skull. Her eyes had a dead stare with that evil sneer still frozen on her mouth. What had happened?

He felt something in his hand. He looked at it. It was an elephant - a book-end figurine of an elephant. It was covered with blood. He dropped it. What had he done?

⁓

"The next thing I knew I was running. I ran until I got here."

"My, my, my, Ben. You sho' got yo'self in a mess. Reminds me of somethin' I read in second chapter of Proverbs - somethin' about "the adulteress, the wayward wife with her seductive words ... her house that leads down to death ..."

Ben wasn't listening. "Ohhhh!" he moaned. "I'm in bad trouble!"

CHAPTER 13

Ben and Isaiah sat quietly for a long time. Finally, Ben broke the silence. "It wasn't my fault!"

"What?"

"It wasn't my fault!" Ben raised his voice.

"What do you mean it weren't your fault?"

"She shouldn't have treated me that way. She shouldn't have said those things about me. She shouldn't have laughed at me."

"Oh! So you get to kill everybody who laughs at you?"

"She just went too far. It's just like all the kids at school. Yeah, that's it!" Ben said. "The kids at school always made fun of me. They laughed. They picked at me. They called me names – just like she did. It's all their fault! They pushed me. They turned me into this … this monster. Why else would I do something like this?" At this point he was talking loudly and pacing.

"Let me get this straight!" Isaiah said. "You killed a girl with a bookend – in her apartment – when the two of you was alone – nobody else around – and it's somebody else's fault?"

"Well, sure! It happens all the time. Don't you watch the news? Columbine. Virginia Tech. It's always the kids everybody picks on that end up killing somebody."

"Son, I think you've been watchin' too much of that television." the old man said. "Did you ever try talkin' to somebody about your problems?"

"Sure. I talked to the teachers. You think they did anything? Hah! They didn't care. And my parents? They just said, 'Toughen up, son'", he imitated his father's gruff voice. "Like that helped!"

"Oh! So, now it's the school's fault, too. And your parents. Ben, you got a bad case of logjam."

"Logjam?"

"Yeah! You know, like when lumberjacks is floating logs down the river to the mill, and the logs get jammed up and can't move."

"What's that got to do with anything?" Ben asked.

"Well, Jesus talked about how we's always lookin' at the splinters in other people's eyes and cain't see the big ole' log in our own eye. When you blame other people for your problems, you got yourself a logjam. Ben, you got to own up to what you done. You cain't blame everybody else! You cain't blame *nobody* else! It was your decision to go home with that girl. It was your decision to let her seduce you. You cain't blame nobody but Ben Wilson."

"I'm not a monster! I never meant to hurt anybody!" Ben yelled.

"No, you ain't no monster. You just the wrong person at the wrong place at the wrong time with the wrong ideas. You made a bad mistake, Ben. But you got to own up to it. It ain't nobody else's fault. If you don't believe in yourself, nobody else is goin' to. But you cain't let their teasin' drive you to doin' wrong."

"It's not fair! What did I do to deserve this?"

"Ben, listen! I ain't sayin' I know how *you* feel. But let me tell you this. I growed up in a little southern town in a time when blacks wasn't welcome in mos' places. I got teased and beat up and 'scriminated against. And yeah, maybe it made me mean. Maybe it drove me to drink. But I cain't blame all those people for what I done. It weren't them that left a dead man layin' in a bar-room floor. It was me. It weren't fair the way they treated me. It was wrong. But I cain't blame them for how a reacted to it. I made a bad decision, and I paid for it with half of my life in prison. Now, that don't make up for what I done. It don't bring back the man I killed. It don't help his family none. But I did my time, and you goin' to have to do yours."

"Humph!" Ben grunted. He didn't have anything else to say. Isaiah wasn't cutting him any slack. So, he withdrew into his pity party and didn't speak again for a long while. Isaiah busied himself with some chores and let Ben stew. And Isaiah prayed.

CHAPTER 14

Sergeant Crowe sent one dog and two officers into the marsh northward, and one dog and two officers southward. He took Officer Lewis with him straight into the marsh headed west. About fifty yards in, he and Lewis noticed some reeds pushed over and lily pads disturbed. He called out for the others to join them. The trail became more noticeable the deeper they went. Again it was obvious that their suspect had no idea how to disguise his path of escape. He was definitely a novice.

They traveled half a mile before they came to dry land again. The dogs rediscovered a scent. They meandered westward for a while, then turned northwest, then south, then east - the guy must have gotten dizzy. Two hours later they were right back in the same place where they picked up the scent.

"Oh boy!" Crowe said to the others, "This could be a long day."

They started out again on the same path, but the men held the dogs at bay while two of the men scouted until they found physical evidence of another route. They repositioned the dogs and got off to another start, hopefully on the right trail this time.

Two more times within the next hour they came to water and had to follow the process of discovery.

It was late afternoon. The two men sat quietly, each thinking about the other man's words.

The old man finally broke the silence, "Ben, you gettin' hungry?"

"Yeah."

"Good! Let's go catch some dinner."

Catch some dinner? At this point Ben was learning just to follow and not question - at least not out loud. The mystery would reveal itself soon enough.

Isaiah went to the side of the cabin, stooped down and reached under the edge. He pulled out two tree limbs approximately six feet long, fairly straight, though not perfect. All the branches had been trimmed and the bark had been skinned off to craft home-made fishing poles. Each one had maybe five feet of clear fishing line tied to the narrow end. At the end of each line was a strange looking hook of some sort - bright silver and 'V' shaped.

"What kind of hooks are these?" Ben asked as Isaiah handed him a pole.

"Well," the old man said, "I kept losin' hooks and straight pins was a lot cheaper. So I just got a box of straight pins, and I bend 'em to make fishhooks. They work pretty good. I lose a fish every once in awhile, but mostly I catch 'em."

"Wow! I would have never thought of that," Ben said, awed at the man's inventiveness. "What about bait? Is there a bait shop out here in the woods?"

"Sho' is," Isaiah said with a wink. "Follow me." He walked thirty yards into the trees, knelt in the dirt, and started digging with his hands. "Well," he called out to Ben, "start shoppin'." He scooped up a handful of dirt and held it up to show three earthworms dangling from the clump. He raked his fingers through and exposed two more.

"Come on, son. These worms ain't gonna dig theirselves."

Ben gaped at him with his mouth half open, eyes wide in wonder.

"Son, you really is a city boy, ain't cha! You never dug worms?"

"Well, yeah, but not for fishing. We just dug them up for fun when I was a kid," Ben said.

"Ain't nothin' fun 'bout diggin' worms ... unless you just like gettin' dirt under your fingernails. This is work ... workin' for food. Now, put your eyes back in your head and your tongue back in mouth, and help me get some fish bait."

Ben got down beside the old man and dug his hands into the dirt. Soon they had a good stock of worms and headed off toward the water. They passed by the cabin and came to a well-worn path leading down the river bank. They walked downstream for a short distance and parked themselves on an oft used tree trunk at the water's edge. Ben sat on the log, then quickly jumped up, backed off a few feet, and examined the log.

"What you doin', boy?" the old man said.

"Oh, I'm just checking for snakes."

Isaiah laughed. "Ben, the snakes are more scared a' you than you are a' them. Ain't no snakes on this log. I sit here most every day. Ain't been bit yet."

Ben eased down onto the log. "Well, that's a relief." He relaxed.

"Now, I ain't saying there ain't no spiders."

Ben jumped back up quickly.

Isaiah let out a big belly laugh. "Son, you as jumpy as a flea on a wet dog. Sit down and start fishin' 'fore the sun goes down."

Ben settled down, but his eyes furtively scanned his surroundings. Snakes, spiders, gators, lizards - he was watching for movement of any kind.

This boy would never survive out here for long. God help him, Isaiah silently prayed.

They sat quietly for a while. Isaiah caught a fish, skillfully shored it and hung it by its gills on a small tree branch nearby. Ben watched spellbound.

This man was truly a descendant of Daniel Boone - well, if Daniel Boone had been black, that is.

After an indeterminate period of silence Ben sighed, "Mr. Isaiah ... I ... I mean, Isaiah."

"Yeah, Ben."

"What am I going to do?"

"Well," he hesitated, "what do you want to do?"

"I want to wake up and find out this is a dream. I want this never to have happened."

"Yeah, I hear you. But that jes' ain't gonna happen. You done what you done, and it ain't gonna go away."

Ben sighed deeply. He sat silently for a while.

Isaiah waited.

Finally Ben spoke again, "What do *you* think I should do?"

Isaiah looked at Ben squarely and spoke slowly and deliberately, "I think you should surrender."

"What? Turn myself in? Isaiah, I killed a woman. I would spend the rest of my life in prison."

"I been there, Ben. Remember? It ain't no fun. But Ben, you cain't run forever. They'll get you sooner or later."

"But how can I just surrender?" Ben said. "And who would I surrender to?"

"Well, that's an interestin' question. I've been thinkin' about that a lot."

"You have? Really?" Ben asked.

"Yeah. Ben, you got to surrender to the police. They gonna be lookin' for ya', and they'll find ya'. You need to jes' walk out of these woods and turn yourself in to the first police man you see. But more important, you need to surrender to God."

"What do you mean?" Ben asked, truly not comprehending what the old man was saying.

"Ben, remember how I tol' you about what happened to me in prison? I turned my life over to Jesus - I surrendered - and he forgave me, saved me, and changed me. Oh, I spent a lotta years behind bars, but in my soul I was free. I don't carry that heavy load a' guilt I used to carry. And now, I can choose the right path and see it through. I'm free from all that drinkin' and fightin' ... free from all that anger and bitterness. I'm free, Ben, free like I never was before. When God sets you free... ahh. Now that's real freedom."

"I'm not sure what all that means. I don't want to become some religious fanatic. I'm not even sure I believe in God ... no offense, I mean —"

"I ain't offended. I'm proud of what God done for me. If I'm a fanatic, so be it. I don't mind bein' called one, if that's what I am. All I know is that I used to be a bad man headed for hell, and now I'm a man forgiven and headed for heaven."

"I hope you're right," Ben said, "but I just don't think I'm ready for that."

"Well now, there's where you have a problem, Ben," Isaiah said.

"What do you mean?"

"Ben, it don't really matter whether you're ready for it or not. It's there. Once you know the truth, you got to make a decision about it."

"What do you mean I've got to make a decision? Why do I *have* to make a decision?"

"Well, when you hear somethin' new, you have to decide whether you believe it or you don't believe it. You either accept it or reject it."

"But what if I choose not to decide?"

"Well now, that's a decision, ain't it, Ben?" Isaiah smiled at him like he was a catfish in a live-well.

Ben was perplexed.

Isaiah pushed on wanting to clarify the point. "Ben, life is kinda like fishin'."

Ben leaned in. "How's that?"

"Well, you want to catch a fish, so you put somethin' on a hook that you think the fish will bite. When he takes the bait, you reel him in and he belongs to ya'."

Ben wrinkled up his face trying to make the connection. A fish tugged at Isaiah's line, but he ignored it, not wanting to distract Ben.

"I don't see —" Ben started.

"God is fishin' for men - you and me. So, he baits his hook, so to speak. He offers you life. He offers all kinds of good things to us ... peace, joy, love, forgiveness ... stuff like that. Good stuff. The Bible is full a' promises. God says in one place, 'I'm settin' before you life and death, and I hope you choose life'. That ain't the exact words, but it's the right meanin'."

"The problem is the devil's fishin', too," he said. "He baits his hook with all the stuff that looks good and seems like fun, but in the end it'll kill you."

"What's wrong with fun?" Ben said, ready to take on the old man..

"Ain't nothin' wrong with fun, boy. It's the things that seem like fun but are deadly that get you."

"Like what?" Ben posed.

"Oh, like if you took some poison and put it in a candy bar so it don't look or taste like poison. Then you'd poison yourself thinkin' you was gettin' a treat. That's what the devil does. He dresses things up so they look like what they ain't."

"So, how do you know the difference? It sounds confusing," Ben confessed. Isaiah sounded convincing, but Ben still didn't understand.

"Well, sometimes it *is* hard to tell the difference. The devil's real tricky. He got us all blinded so we cain't tell the difference 'tween truth 'n lies ... 'tween good 'n bad, wrong 'n right. But if you listen real hard, you can hear God callin'. When you surrender to him, he makes it clearer. See, you cain't understand 'til God opens your eyes."

"Well, I don't —" Ben started to say.

"Just think on it, Ben. Tha's all I ask."

"Yeah, I'll try to keep an open mind. But I just don't get this surrender thing."

"Ben," Isaiah said, "you cain't run forever ... from God or from the law."

Just then Ben felt a tug on his fishing line.

"Well Ben, looks like you got a decision to make," Isaiah said.

"What?"

"You got a fish tuggin' on your line. Now, you gotta decide whether you gonna reel him in or let him get away ... or whether you gonna jes' sit there 'n let *him* decide."

Isaiah got up to leave.

Ben just sat there bewildered.

The fish got away.

CHAPTER 15

Isaiah sat down on a stump behind a rugged table outside the cabin. He pulled out a knife and started cleaning one of the two fish he had caught. Two fish were enough for two men. The fishing was really more about the conversation anyway. Isaiah was fishing, but not just for the ones in the river. He was on God's fishing expedition, and Ben was the intended catch.

Ben meandered in empty handed but deep in thought.

"You ever clean a fish, Ben?"

"Yeah, a couple of times. Didn't much like it."

"Ain't much to like 'cept the eatin' when it's done," the old man said without looking up. "Get yourself a knife out of the cabin and clean that fish there. The Bible says, 'if a man don't work, he don't eat'. So, tonight you get to work for your supper." He flashed Ben a big smile.

Ben went in to find a knife. He returned and dutifully cleaned his fish. In the end, Isaiah had a beautifully filleted fish. Ben had a pile of mutilated fish meat.

Isaiah took the fish into the kitchen and began preparations for a fish fry. He sent Ben out to the pump to get some water.

Ben had never seen a hand-operated water pump before, but he quickly figured out how to extract water from the antique contraption. He pushed down on the handle. That much was obvious. At first nothing happened. After a couple of pumps he heard a gurgle. Then water started gushing.

He came in with a big bucket of water. Isaiah was firing up the old dual-burner campstove. He took the water and put some in two saucepans. In one he cooked rice, and in the other, he poured a can of pinto beans. He added a little fatback for flavor.

He then started a fire in the fireplace. He already had everything set up - the firewood, the kindling, and the matches. Ben was amazed at the old man's efficiency in the little homestead.

When he got the fire going, Isaiah grabbed an old wrought iron frying pan, picked up a worn coffee can, and poured out some grease that looked like it had been reused at least fifty times. It had. At least. Soon the smell of frying fish filled the tiny cabin.

Within thirty minutes supper was on the table. Isaiah sent Ben back out to fill two glasses with fresh water from the pump. He stirred in a little instant tea and some sugar, and they sat down to eat. There wasn't much conversation. Ben was still deep in thought. He had some big decisions to make, and he didn't want to make any of them. Isaiah was silently praying for his young friend.

Darkness settled in. Isaiah lit up the kerosene lantern and prepared for bed. Ben was amazed at the early American flavor of everything about the cabin. It reminded him of the memorabilia in the dining area of a Cracker Barrel restaurant. Only this stuff was still in use - and there was no waitress. Isaiah sat on his thick padded chair and took off his shirt. The man was as lean and bony as anyone Ben had ever seen. He turned away to give Isaiah privacy. Then a thought struck him.

"Isaiah," Ben said as he turned to face the man. When he looked at the old man he gasped and stumbled back onto the bed, nearly falling onto the floor. He struggled to regain his composure but was not very successful. He shook his head and closed and reopened his eyes several times to be sure he was seeing correctly.

Isaiah sat on the edge of his chair with the bottom part of his left leg, knee to foot, at eye level, in both hands, examining his shoe.

Ben looked down at the empty pant leg and took a deep breath. This all seemed to happen in slow motion.

"Yeah?" Isaiah said as he looked up. He caught the shocked look on Ben's face.

"How? ... What? ... Why? ..." Ben sputtered. "I mean ... I didn't know —"

"Oh, I shoulda tol' you 'fore you turned around. I guess it's kind a shock when you don't see it comin'." Isaiah blushed, if a man that dark can blush.

"What happened, Gator? Crock?" Ben asked.

"Remember I tol' you about when I got arrested. Well, I tried to run away. It was around Thanksgiving ... late '50s. There was snow on the ground and it was below zero."

"Snow? In the lowcountry?"

"It don't happen often, but it did that night. They called it a 'blockbustin' freeze 'cause the engine blocks in a lot of cars froze up and busted that night. I was at my mama's house hidin' out. When I heard the cops comin', I ran. My mama begged me not to. She was afraid they would kill me, bein' a young black man and all.

"I panicked. I ran out the back and into the woods as fast and as far as I could go. I ran for two days. Give 'em a good chase. But in the freezin', wet swamp I got frostbite. When they caught me, I was layin' on the ground unable to move. I couldn't feel my legs ... couldn't feel much of anything. They took me to the hospital, did everything they could, but they couldn't save the foot. I lost half of my leg and half of my life that weekend, Ben."

CHAPTER 16

"Give me some good news, Ross!" Detective Jones spoke into his cell phone. Jones was calling from the Police Sub-station in Murrells Inlet. Lt. John Ross was in his car in the parking lot of the golf course near the cornfield where they had begun the canine search. He was staying close to the soft drink machines on this sultry August day.

"Nothing yet, Boss. The dogs have been on the trail a few hours. They lost the scent a few times because of the water, but they're back on it the last I heard," Ross reported.

"And when's the last you heard?" Jones asked.

"About forty-five minutes ago."

"Well, call them back. I want an up to the minute report."

"Okay, George ... I mean, Boss. I'll get right back with you." He ended the call and dialed Sgt. Crowe.

"Yeah! What's up, John?" Crowe spoke into his speaker phone.

"That's what I'm calling to ask you," Ross said. "Jones wants an up-to-the-minute progress report."

"Well, we're still tracking. The dogs seem to have a good take on the scent. No more problems since the last time we talked. But John, it's getting dark out here fast. It's not safe to keep moving through this swampy wood at night, what with all the snakes and gators and such. I don't want to put my guys at risk. We're going have to stop."

"Yeah, I thought about that. Are you prepared —?"

Crowe cut him off, "John, don't insult me again. Each of us has a backpack containing a light weight one man tent – and one of those Mylar blanket things, you know. We got flashlights, hunting knives - those Rambo kinds with the compass and all, like we need that," he chuckled. "And each of us has some crackers, a can of Viennas, and a can of Beanie Weenies."

"Hmm! Sounds like a blast - no pun intended."

"Yeah, right!" Crowe said. "And we've got plenty of matches - water-proof, of course, and ... Oh yeah ... snake repellent."

"Snake repellent?" Ross said, scratching his head.

"I've got my side-arm with me." He patted his hoslter. "And I'm quicker on the draw than any water moccasin I've come across yet," Crowe said.

"Well! You're a regular cowboy, Crowe. Yeehah! You're a good man, Harry."

"Why thank ya' Sheriff. Oh, and John, one more thing."

"Yeah, what is it Sarge?"

"Given our location and the direction we're headed, I think I have an idea where we might find this kid."

"Really?" Ross sat up. Crowe had his attention. "Where?"

"There's an old man, an ex-con, who stays in a cabin a couple of miles northwest of our present location, if my calculations are correct. It looks like the suspect was headed in that direction. He might have stumbled onto the cabin and could be holed up there. I just hope if that's the case, he hasn't hurt the old man - Isaiah, I think his name is."

"You think the old guy might be helping him?" Ross asked.

"No, not in the way you're thinking. Old Isaiah got religious in prison. He's harmless. He took up the life of a hermit for some reason when he got out. But I don't think he'd help the suspect escape. If anything, he'll probably try to covert him."

"Good! Then maybe he'll find Jesus and turn himself in, and we'll all celebrate over brunch sometime in the morning," Ross said, though with some skepticism. "Ya'll be safe, and sleep tight."

"Yeah!" Crowe said with a grin. "Well be staying at the Francis Marion National Forest Hilton if you need us! Over and out!"

Sergeant Harry Crowe was a good man - the best. He'd lived in Georgetown county all of his life. He had a little place in Pawley's Island, a beach house his parents left him. The house had been in the family for generations. Harry was as thorough and as honest as they come - a small town boy with small town values. If anybody could track this kid through the swamps of Georgetown County, Harry Crowe could.

Happy hunting, Harry.

Ross immediately called Detective Jones.

"Hey boss. The dogs are still on the trail. They haven't caught up with him yet, but Sgt. Crowe thinks he might have an idea. There's an old ex-con who stays in a cabin out in the woods near here. Crowe thinks the trail is leading that way. Odds are if the suspect found the cabin, he might be holed up there - maybe even holding the old guy hostage."

"Any possibility the old man is helping him, being an ex-con, I mean?" Jones asked.

"Crowe doesn't think so. The old man got religion, and Crowe thinks he's straight up. He doesn't think he'd do anything outside of the law," Ross answered.

"Well, you never know. Tell them to proceed with caution. We don't know if the suspect is armed or not. Maybe the old hermit has a gun on the premises. We don't want any officers or the old man hurt."

"Right boss! I'll relay your concern," Ross assured him.

"Hey Ross, it's starting to get dark. Probably darker in the deep woods. Are those guys going to be okay out there?"

"I was going to mention that. Crowe says it's too dangerous to keep moving in that swampy area at night. They're gonna camp tonight and pick it back up at dawn."

"Yeah, that's what I was thinking. Do they have what they need?"

"Hey," Ross said, "We're talking about Harry Crowe here. He's a regular Boy Scout - always prepared, you know. He's probably got a Pawley's Island hammock in his backpack. Or maybe he'll just weave one out of swamp grass. He's probably hanging between a couple of oak trees snoring by now."

Jones chuckled, "Well, I hope so. Call me if you hear anything, John."

"Will do, Jonesy! I'll be sleeping in my car so I can stay close to the action in case anything develops. Good night."

"Ross, you're top notch."

"Thanks George!"

Officer Simmons entered the room where Jones was just shutting off his phone. "Hey, Jonesy. What's the progress on the Fairfax murder?"

"Oh, we're tracking our suspect. We won't really know much more until we get him in custody."

"Well, good luck with that. I'm heading home. You need anything?" Simmons offered.

"No, but thanks. You have a good night."

Simmons walked out to his car and drove away.

Jones leaned back in his chair and closed his eyes.

CHAPTER 17

Ben stepped out into the morning sun, what little of it was peeking through the thickness of the forest. Two lizards were poised at the front of the cabin with their backs arched enjoying the rays of the sun. They looked like little soldiers standing at attention - guarding Ben's tiny fortress in the woods. He listened to the gentle chirping of the frogs, the whispering of the wind through the trees, the slight rustling of the leaves, the unfamiliar and varied sounds of the swamp. It was comforting, even peaceful, in the midst of his current crisis. Then came another sound that brought a cloud of dread - the distant barking of dogs.

"Oh God! They're coming!" he screamed. He looked around in every direction checking for signs of his pursuers, or maybe trying to plan his escape. Isaiah couldn't tell which.

"What you thinkin', boy?" the old man asked. "Don't run, Ben," he reminded him. "Surrender."

"I ... I can't." Ben cried, his throat filled with panic. "I've got to get away from here. Which way, Isaiah? Which way should I go?"

"I say you go straight into their hands if ya' know what's good for ya'," Isaiah insisted.

"No! No! I can't do that."

With that said, Ben bolted into the forest in the opposite direction of the sound of the approaching dogs. He ran with all his might, over this fallen tree trunk, under that one, around this bush and then another, through the dangling moss, tripping several times over fallen tree limbs and stumps.

"Foolish, son," Isaiah muttered to himself. "Real foolish."

Within moments howling dogs broke through the underbrush dragging harried officers behind them. Isaiah stood at the front of his cabin and watched them approach. The dogs were sniffing the ground excitedly as they sensed a fresh trail. They pulled furiously at their leashes, eager to pursue their prey.

Sgt. Crowe called out to Isaiah, "Is he here?"

The old man shook his head and answered sadly, "He ran. I tried to talk him out of it." He just continued to shake his head and stare at the ground.

"I figured as much," Crowe said. "Did he hurt you?"

"No. He's harmless. Just scared."

"Which way did he go? You'd might as well tell us. You know we'll catch him eventually. Don't try to protect him."

Isaiah pointed into the forest behind the cabin. He didn't offer comment. He just pointed.

"How long ago?" Crowe asked. The others were trying to control the dogs.

"Couple of minutes," Isaiah said. "He won't get far."

"No! He won't!" Crowe responded. "Go!" he ordered as he pointed in the direction Isaiah had indicated.

Ben ran hard but kept getting tangled in the weeds and the mud, like one of those dreams where you try to run but your legs won't work. He tripped and lunged headfirst into a thick patch of kudzu. As he tried to get up he found his legs were tangled in the vines. He could hear the dogs getting closer. He kicked and pulled until he finally broke free. It took a couple of minutes. He got to his knees and attempted to stand up and run. But when he got to his feet he looked up and found himself surrounded by six police officers with guns drawn and aimed straight at him.

"Give it up, son," the lead officer said. "I'm Sgt. Harry Crowe with the Georgetown County Police Department. You're under arrest for the murder of Elizabeth Fairfax of Murrells Inlet. If you have any weapons, lay them on the ground now, and put your hands in the air where I can see them."

Ben slowly looked around at the men surrounding him. "Don't shoot," he said as he put up his hands. "I'm not armed. Please, don't shoot me. And keep those dogs back." Ben started to cry.

"Are you Benjamin Wilson?" Crowe asked.

"Yes," Ben whimpered, his bottom lip trembling.

"Cuff him!" Crowe told one of the officers standing by. "And read him his rights."

Then he turned back to Ben. "Son, I'm tired. I'm hungry. I'm sleepy. I'm wet. And I'm cranky. So, don't give me any trouble. You've put me and my men through a rough night, so, don't provoke me."

Ben didn't have to be told twice.

Sgt. Harry Crowe was a tall, muscular man with a tough look. He wouldn't hurt a flea except in self-defense, but Ben didn't know that. And that was the way Crowe wanted it.

Officer Franky Marsh put the cuffs on Ben as he began to recite, "Benjamin Wilson, you are under arrest for the murder of Elizabeth Fairfax. You have the right to remain silent ..."

Ben didn't hear the rest. His world was reeling. They led him out of the woods. As they passed Isaiah's cabin the old man stood watching with tears in his eyes. Ben looked at him pleadingly like a lost puppy.

Sgt. Crowe took the shortest route to the road and sent two of the men to get the police van and his squad car. He explained to them where to meet him. He knew these woods well. It was slow going with a handcuffed prisoner, but at least this part of the ordeal was nearly over.

CHAPTER 18

It took two hours to get out of the woods to the paved road leading back to Murrells Inlet. When Sgt. Crowe, his prisoner, three dogs and three men got to the meeting place, the van and squad car were waiting for them. They arrived at the sub-station just before noon and were greeted by Detective Jones. He eyed his suspect but didn't speak to him. He pulled Sgt. Crowe aside and got the details of the capture.

"Harry, I'm going to have to ask you to bring Mr. Washington in for questioning. We need to find out what he knows. Maybe Wilson gave him some information that will help with our investigation."

"Sure," Crowe said. "When do you want him?"

"The sooner the better, I guess. Give me some time to question the suspect and then I need to find out what Mr. Washington knows."

"Okay. How about I go get something to eat and wash off a little, and then I'll take Marsh with me and go back out and get Washington?" Crowe suggested.

"No," Jones said. "You go get a hot meal, a hot bath, and a couple of hours sleep, and then go get him later this afternoon. I don't suppose there's any way to let him know you're coming," he half commented, half questioned.

"Well, I could send up a smoke signal," the Sergeant joked.

"From what I hear you probably could," Jones said. "Just call me on your way in so I can prepare for him."

"Got it! Thanks, Jonesy!" With that Crowe was off, but not before communicating with Officer Marsh what the plan was for the afternoon. He sent the rest of the team home.

〰

Ben was ushered into a small bathroom where he was able to sponge bathe while the guard waited outside the door. He was given a jail uniform, and his clothes were tagged and bagged - with a note to clean the swamp smell off of them as soon as possible. Then Ben was seated in the interrogation room – not a sophisticated one with a one-way mirror like they have on all the cop shows. But it did have a plain table and a couple of chairs, just like on TV. Jones let him sit for about an hour before entering the room. Then he walked in and gave Ben a few minutes to size him up.

"Mr. Wilson," he began, "I'm Detective Jones. I would like for you to tell me where you were at one clock on Saturday afternoon?"

Ben sat quietly, defiantly staring at the floor.

"Mr. Wilson," he tried again, "you want to tell me what happened at Elizabeth Fairfax's apartment on Saturday?"

Still no response.

"Listen, son, don't make this harder than it has to be. We have your fingerprints in Miss Fairfax's apartment and on the murder weapon – you do remember the murder weapon don't you?" He was hoping to get Ben to say something to incriminate himself. "We have your DNA from Miss Fairfax's lips. And we have a witness that saw a man matching your description fleeing the scene of the crime. We have an open and shut case without your cooperation. You might as well tell me what happened."

Ben maintained his silence. His face was turning red. Jones couldn't tell if it was embarrassment, anger, or just stubbornness causing him to blush. He waited. Twenty minutes passed with no comment.

Finally Jones blew out a puff of air. "Okay, have it your way, kid. You can sit here until you decide to cooperate." With that he left the room.

Officer Simmons was in the main office. "You don't look like you had too much success. Suspect not cooperating?"

"No, he wants to be a hard case!" Jones spit the words out in frustration.

"Or maybe he's just afraid, or confused," Simmons suggested.

"Yeah, could be," Jones conceded. "Cal, how about get the kid a sandwich and a coke, would you?"

"Sure. What kind of Coke?" Simmons asked.

"What do you mean 'what kind of coke?' - diet, cherry, I don't care. What kind of question is that?"

Simmons blushed. "Sorry boss. Just slipped out. See, my family refers to all soft drinks as 'a coke'. It's just something I grew up with." He grinned.

"Real cute," Jones said. "Any flavor he wants. Find out what he would like, and be a good boy and get it for him, will ya'."

Simmons went in and talked with Ben.

Jones sat down to make some notes.

Simmons came out and reported to the detective. "Sweet tea!" he quipped, "And a Reuben sandwich!"

Jones rolled his eyes. "Oh, give me a break."

Simmons stood there with a questioning look awaiting further instructions.

"Okay! Okay! Get him a Reuben and a tea. What are we running here, a catering service?" He handed Simmons some petty cash out of the safe box in the desk drawer and signed it out in the log book. "Of all the cockamamie requests! When's the last time anybody ordered a Reuben sandwich around here?"

Simmons laughed as he left the squad room.

It was mid-afternoon. Ben had eaten his Reuben sandwich. He had made a trip to the bathroom and laid his head on the table and fallen asleep from boredom. Detective Jones decided to try again to question him. He entered the room noisily to let Ben know he had come in. He repositioned his chair - turned it around, straddled it, and leaned forward putting his elbows on the chair back, and dangling his arms in front of him. He glared at Ben.

"Mr. Wilson, are you ready to talk to me?"

Ben rubbed the sleep out of his eyes and, again, stared at the floor. He grunted, but said nothing intelligible.

"Son, I don't know what you expect to gain by being a hard case. All you're going to accomplish is to put everybody in a bad mood and make people reluctant to be objective. We can help you or hurt you, you know. All we want is the truth. We're going to find out anyway. You might as well talk to me."

"I got nothing to say," Ben scowled.

"Well, that just means that we'll have to assume our best guess about what happened. The circumstantial evidence points to you as a murderer. You can help yourse—"

"I'm not a murderer," Ben yelled.

"Well, now that's a start," Jones said, hoping that Ben was ready to open up. "You want to tell me what happened?"

"No! Like I said, I got nothing to say."

"Okay, have it your way. I'll be talking to Mr. Washington soon."

"Who?" Ben snapped.

"Mr. Washington. The man at the cabin."

"Isaiah?" Ben asked. He seemed agitated.

"Yes, Isaiah. And trust me, son, if he knows anything, we'll get it out of him."

"Yeah, you're just like everybody else. Out to get me! Why should you be any different?"

"Son, you've got a real chip on your shoulder, and I can tell you, that attitude won't get you anything but trouble," Jones spit the words out and left the room.

⟳

Sergeant Crowe brought Isaiah Washington into the Murrells Inlet Police Sub-station and had him take a seat. He informed Detective Jones that they had arrived.

"You got plans for tonight, Harry?" Jones asked.

"I was kind of hoping to take my wife to church," Crowe answered. "There's a special concert tonight at our church - some family group from Macedonia."

"Really? Wow!" Jones remarked, truly impressed. "Do they sing in English or in ... ummm ... what language do they speak in Macedonia?"

Crowe suppressed a laugh. "Uh! I don't really know for sure what language they speak in Macedonia ... Macedonian would be my guess. But, George, these people are from Macedonia, South Carolina. It's a little country town between Andrews and Monck's Corner."

"Oh! ... Never heard of it," Jones admitted, totally embarrassed. "Well, Harry, go take your wife to church. We've got things covered here. Can you make it in time?"

"Yeah, it starts at seven thirty. Thanks, Jonesy. Oh! What about Mr. Washington?"

"I'll take him back myself when we're through. Do you think he will be okay to walk from the road to his cabin in the dark?"

"Yeah. He knows that place like the back of his hand. He'll be okay. I hope he is helpful," Crowe said.

"Oh, he will be ... one way or another."

CHAPTER 19

"Hello, Mr. Washington," Jones greeted the old man. "I'm Detective Jones."

"Yeah, the other police man tol' me." Isaiah responded matter-of-factly.

"I appreciate your coming in to talk with me tonight," Jones said.

"It ain't like I had much choice!" Isaiah grumbled.

"Well, still, I appreciate any help you can give us. I hope we haven't inconvenienced you too much." Jones was really trying to get in the old man's good graces. He needed his cooperation, and he hoped to get it voluntarily. But he would play hardball if he had to.

Isaiah didn't lighten up. "I don't much like comin' into town. I prefer the gators and the critters to people." Then he added, "I ain't had no supper neither." Now *he* was playing hardball.

Jones smiled broadly. "Well, Mr. Washington, I think we can take care of that. What would you like? You just tell me, and I'll have it brought in as soon as possible."

Isaiah thought for a minute. Finally he spoke, "Well, I ain't had no fried okra in a while ... and some mashed taters with gravy ... uhmmm ... and some fried chicken livers. Umm hmmm! It's been a mighty long while."

Isaiah looked at the detective like he really didn't expect his request to be honored.

"Mmm! Mmm! Mmm! Mr. Washington. You do have good taste. I think I'll order that for two."

"I don't much like bein' called Mister neither. Isaiah'll do jes' fine."

"You got it. How about I call you Ike? How would that be?" Jones asked.

"My mama didn't like the name Ike. She called me Isaiah. That's what folks call me. Jes' plain Isaiah. That's what I want to be called."

Jones gritted his teeth. This was one tough old buzzard. "Okay, Isaiah. Let's step into this room over here and talk."

"Yeah! I been in a room like that before ... long time ago."

Jones sent an officer to the Cracker Barrel over on Route 17 for the food.

⌒

"Now, Isaiah, I suggest you tell us what you know, or —."

Isaiah broke in, "Now, ain't no cause to threaten me, Mister. I got no reason to hide nothin'. I tried to tell that boy he cain't run. I'll tell you what he told me. I ain't gonna break no laws."

"Good!" Jones sighed. "So, what did Mr. Wilson ... uh ... Ben, tell you? Please tell me everything."

Isaiah related his conversation with Ben as best he could remember. Jones wrote everything down and had Isaiah read it and sign it. He was actually surprised that Isaiah could read and write given his background. He learned, upon asking about it, that Isaiah had never had any formal education as a child, because he had to work to help support the family. As a boy he worked alongside his parents in tobacco fields in North Carolina, cotton fields in South Carolina, and peanut farms in Georgia. He learned to read in prison. He learned other things, too. The old man might be uneducated, but he wasn't dumb. He was very thorough in his recollection of Ben's confession. Of course, this was second-hand information, but it would give the detective some leverage when he talked with Ben again.

Jones thanked Isaiah for his help. Conveniently, the food came just as they were finishing. Jones and Washington ate at the same table at which they had talked. Isaiah had softened, captivated by Jones' winning personality, no doubt. Then they climbed into a squad car and headed back to a point on the road where Isaiah could trek back to his cabin.

As they traveled the fifteen minutes to the drop-off site, they talked about growing up in the low-country. They actually had a lot in common aside from the racial differences. As Isaiah got out of the vehicle Jones asked again if he would be okay walking through the swampy forest alone at night.

Isaiah said, "Detective, let me tell you a story. They was three preachers fishin' in a boat. The Pentecostal preacher says, 'Oh, I forgot my bait.' So, he steps outta the boat and walks to the shore and comes back with his tackle box. The other two preachers looks at one another, and the Methodist preacher says to the Baptist preacher, 'If he can do that, so can we.' Well, they steps outta the boat and sinks plumb to the bottom. So, they climbs back in the boat, and they looks at the Pentecostal preacher and they say, 'How did you do that?' And the Pentecostal preacher, why he smiles and he says, 'I knows where the rocks is.'"

Jones laughed politely. He had heard the joke before. "So, the point is?" he asked.

Isaiah grinned. His white teeth seemed to glow in the black background of his face and the darkness of the night. "In these woods, I knows where the rocks is!" With that he turned toward the swampy forest. He took a few steps and turned back, "Oh, and detective, next time you get a hankerin' for fried chicken livers and okra, I'll be glad to join you."

Jones called back, "You can count on it!" Then he drove off into the night.

The following morning, Jones had Ben brought back into the interrogation room. He had been put into a holding cell overnight.

"Good morning, Mr. Wilson, did you sleep well?" Jones asked.

"That bed is worse than the one in Isaiah's cabin," he groused.

"Well, that's why we call it jail, son. It's made for punishment - not for comfort. It amazes me how criminals complain about being treated like criminals. You just can't find any grateful criminals these days." He had dropped the cheeriness and resumed his sarcasm. "I had an interesting conversation with your friend. Isaiah, last night. He told me everything."

"Then he's not my friend if he sold me out," Ben said, obviously hurt and feeling betrayed.

"Son, there's two things you've got to realize. First of all, if Mr. Washington hadn't told me, he could be charged with aiding and abetting a criminal. Do you know what that means? He would be as guilty as you are, and he would go back to prison."

"Secondly, Washington may be the best friend you've got right now. He wouldn't have helped you by lying for you. That's not real friendship. Do you know that old man cried for you while he was talking to me last night? He really seems to care what happens to you. And he knows from experience that you have to face the consequences for your actions. He did, and he's a better man for it today."

"He told me he's a better man because he got religious."

"Well, I'm sure that didn't hurt," Jones responded. "But a man does a lot of thinking when he's behind bars. He has time to evaluate his life, his actions, and his place in the world. And he has time to think about the ramifications of what he's done and what he's going to do. A lot of them stay the same and become career criminals and perpetual prisoners. Some, like Isaiah decide to change. He wants to give you that chance.

"You killed that girl, Elizabeth Fairfax. We know that. We know how you killed her. That much is obvious. What we don't know is why you killed her and if anyone else was involved. You might help yourself by talking to me."

"What does it matter?" Ben spit it out. "You're going to put me in prison either way. You're just going to do what everybody always does - just get rid of the misfit, the ugly kid with the big ears and the dull personality."

"Ben, you've got a lot of anger, son. I don't know what's made you so angry, but I've seen what anger can turn a man into. I've put away a lot of criminals in my time. Most of them were angry just like you. But, when you get to prison, that anger will be replaced by fear. You'll find men who are bigger, meaner, and angrier than you are."

"Yeah, and they'll all pick on me, and push me around, and make fun of me like everybody always has."

"Oh, they'll do more than push you around and make fun of you. A lot more," Jones said.

Ben bit his now trembling lip. The fear was already creeping up on him.

"Ben, I've seen a lot of men like you. They all feel like they are victims instead of offenders. They all blame somebody else for their lot in life. I'll bet you think other people made you do this, because they pushed you and made fun of you and rejected you."

"You sound like Isaiah now!" Ben snapped.

"Yeah? What did he say?" Jones raised an eyebrow.

"Oh, something about how everybody has it tough, and we all make our own decisions about how we deal with it, and it's not other people's fault that we make bad choices," Ben said.

"Sounds like a wise man."

"Well, still, he wasn't there and neither were you."

"So, you admit that you were there in Miss Fairfax's apartment, the young lady who was murdered."

"Yeah, I was there. But I wouldn't call her a lady. She was evil," Ben spewed out the words like venom.

"Oh, *she* was evil. I suppose you believe it's *her* fault she's dead."

"It *is* her fault!" Ben shouted. He slammed his fists on the table. "She wouldn't stop! She just kept laughing at me - mocking me - calling me names. I begged her to stop ... and then ... and then she stopped." He stared blankly as the memory swept over him.

"Tell me what happened, son," Jones spoke softly.

"I ... I ... don't know," Ben stammered. "She came on to me. She took me to her place. She led me on. Pretended she liked me. Then she humiliated me. She kept laughing that evil laugh ... calling me terrible things. She kept on and on and on. I told her to stop. I begged her to. Then ... I ... I don't know. Everything kinda went black. Then it got quiet. And when I looked around, she was dead."

"You don't remember picking up the bookend and hitting her?" Jones asked.

"No! I remember the bookend. It was an elephant. It was ... in ... my hand." Ben had a distant look like he was trying to remember. "I dropped it when I saw her on the floor, and I ran."

"And you don't remember picking it up and hitting her."

"No! But you should have heard the things she was saying to me ... the way she was ridiculing me ... she was cruel ... just like all the others."

"Ben, was anyone else in the room?" the detective asked.

"No! We were alone. I thought ... thought I was going to ... I thought we were going to ..." he trailed off.

"Son, I know it must have been very traumatic. But you should have just left the apartment. That would have had a much better ending."

"I ... I killed her?" Ben's mouth dropped open wide.

"Your prints were on the bookend that smashed her skull, Ben. Yeah! It looks like you killed her."

"I killed somebody. I killed her." Ben continued to repeat the phrase robotically as the reality sank in. He already knew it, but he hadn't actually faced the reality of it until this moment. It had seemed like a dream ... or something that had happened to somebody else, but somehow he knew it firsthand. Now, it hit him full-force. "I killed somebody," he whimpered.

The guards led him back to his cell. The next day he was transferred to the Georgetown County Jail to await official charging and sentencing. Detective George Jones and Officer Cal Simmons witnessed his signed confession.

CHAPTER 20

The Georgetown County Jail was larger than the Murrell's Inlet substation, but the cell was pretty much the same. From the small window Ben could stand on tip-toes and catch a glimpse of the Georgetown waterfront - an inlet of the Winyah Bay. The waterfront was almost completely blocked from view by the shops along Front Street. But behind the shops was a boardwalk with benches and tables where shoppers and tourists could enjoy a snack or a beverage and feel the gentle ocean breeze as it wafted across the bay. Shrimp boats and a few small yachts were moored on the docks along the waterfront like a scene from a Thomas Kinkade painting.

Ben watched the billowing smoke from the steel mill, and beyond that, the smoke and the smell of the paper mill. Ben's grandfather had moved the family to Georgetown in the late 1940's to work at the world's largest paper mill. He could smell the strong scent of the slow cooking wood pulp drifting from the mill in the process of making paper. Visitors to the town would complain of the awful smell, but Ben's grandmother always said, "That smells like money to me."

Ben smiled as he thought about his childhood home on South Island Road where he had lived with his parents and his younger sister, Patsy. His grandparents lived next door, and the neighborhood consisted mostly of relatives. The awareness that he would never again visit the places of his childhood haunted him.

Ben's reverie was interrupted by the rattling of keys. He was getting a cell-mate. A scruffy man in his mid-thirties was led into the cell. An officer took him by the shoulders and sat him down on the bed and promptly left.

"Hi, my name is Jer-ry," the man finally said.

Ben tried to ignore him.

"What's your name?" Jerry wore a big grin and had a far-off look in his eyes.

"Ben."

Jerry sat upright, stiff-backed on the edge of his bed with his hands folded in his lap. He fidgeted constantly.

"What are you in jail for?" Jerry asked.

"What?" Ben half-shouted.

"What are you in jail for?"

"None of your business."

"Oh!" Jerry said. "I unirated on the sidewalk."

"You what?" Ben glared at Jerry in unbelief.

"I unirated on the sidewalk," Jerry repeated. "I was in front of the Town Clock on Front Street, and I had to go. The police told me I shouldn't do that, but I couldn't wait."

Ben rolled his eyes. "You're in jail because you u-ri-nated on the sidewalk?"

"Yeah, in front of the Town Clock. It's the oldest building in Georgetown? But they rebuilt it in 1842 'cause it was getting old."

Ben grunted.

"You want me to tell you about Georgetown? I know all about it."

"No," Ben said, But Jerry didn't seem to notice.

"Georgetown is one of the oldest towns in the South - even in the whole country."

"Really," Ben said in a flat, deadpan tone.

"They used to grow Indigo here. I never saw Indigo before. Have you?"

Ben said nothing.

"I read that they made dye from Indigo."

Ben remained silent.

"Then they grew rice here, and they made slaves work in the fields. And then they cut down trees and made wood, and now they make paper."

"Jerry, what in the world are you talking about - they cut down trees and made wood?"

"You know! Boards! For building houses and stuff. But they don't make boards anymore. Now they make paper, you know, at the paper mill."

"Fascinating." Ben feigned a yawn.

"Did you know that two of the men who signed the Declaration of Independence lived in Geor—?"

"Jerry, I don't care! Just be quiet."

"Okay."

Jerry sat quietly for a few minutes. Ben watched him, hoping he would stay that way. Long minutes passed.

"Thomas Lynch."

"What?" Ben snapped.

"Thomas Lynch. He signed the Declaration of Independence. And his son. They were from Georgetown."

"Jer-ry, shut up! Take a nap or something!"

Jerry put on a silly grin, bobbed his head a couple of times, and then said, "Okay." He laid across the bunk and within minutes was snoring.

Ben looked at him with amazement. *Wow! Life must be easy for the simple-minded.*

He climbed up on the top bunk and stretched out. Soon he drifted off to sleep as well. He dreamed about his childhood. He and his cousins were climbing in the great sycamore tree in his grandparent's front yard. They were stripping sheets of bark from that tree trying to see who could peel the largest section without breaking it. That tree looked like a wounded leper when those boys left it.

Then they chased each other through the acres of soft pine straw that covered the ground beneath the tall southern pines in the woods nearby. They wrestled for hours. Then grandmamma called them in for some fresh fig preserves she had just made.

∽

Ben woke up to find Jerry sitting stiff-backed on the edge of the bed again. Ben hopped down from the bunk.

"You're awake," Jerry said.

"You're a genius," Ben mumbled.

"Have you ever been to the Kaminski House? Lafayette lived there in the Revolutionary War. He was from France."

Oh great! Here we go on the history of Georgetown again.

"Do you want me to tell you about Lafayette?"

"Not really," Ben said.

"He was a French General or something. I think he helped Francis Marion fight. You heard of Francis Marion?"

"The Swamp Fox."

"Yeah. I wonder why they called him a swamp fox."

"Well, probably because he hid in the swamps, and he was smart like a fox."

"Really?"

"Yeah, he led military campaigns in the swamps between Charleston and Georgetown. Marion was famous for ambushing British troops and then disappearing into the swamps. He completely disoriented the British."

"Hey, I saw this movie —"

"The Patriot, with Mel Gibson."

"Yeah, but they called him something else, but I think it was Francis Marion."

"Yeah, me too." Ben said.

Moments passed.

Finally Ben said, "You know, when I was a kid we used to pretend we were swamp foxes fighting the British."

"That sounds like fun," Jerry said.

"Then we would pull big clumps of moss off of oak trees and drape it over our heads and chase each other like monsters."

Jerry bounced up and down and clapped his hands. "That's funny," he giggled.

"Yeah," Ben said. "Those were good times."

Jerry was still bouncing. "My parents used to take me to Pawley's Island. They've got Palmetto trees there. It looks like Hawaii or something. We ate pimento cheese sandwiches, and I got sand in my teeth."

Ben's imagination flashed to one of the many family picnics he attended on the beaches of Pawley's Island. He could almost feel the hot sand under his feet, the splash of the surf against his legs - could almost hear the soft crashing of the waves - taste the salty spray of the ocean water - feel the grit of sand in his mouth.

Then reality crashed in on him again. He would never experience these things again. His mood quickly soured.

"Jerry, I don't want to talk anymore."

"But this is fun. I want to hear some more stories."

"Just leave me alone."

Jerry pouted for while and then went back to sleep.

Ben paced the small cell for a while - three steps this way, then back, then back again. Then Ben Wilson made a decision that would dramatically upset business-as-usual in the Georgetown judicial system.

CHAPTER 21

Ben appeared before Judge Lawrence Miller. The judge rapped his gavel on the desk to begin the business at hand. He cleared his throat. "Benjamin Frederick Wilson, I have in my hand a signed confession that you willfully and maliciously took the life of - murdered - Elizabeth Fairfax at her apartment on Route 17 in Murrells Inlet on the date of August 14, 1999. Do you stand by this confession, or do you wish to contest it?"

Ben answered with measured confidence, "I ... I stand by my confession sir. I ... am ..." he barely squeezed the word out, "guilty."

Ben's mother let out a yelp. Tears were pouring down her cheeks. She had tried not to believe it. Her son - a murderer. She had hoped beyond hope that it was not true, but now she heard it from his own lips. His father sat stone-faced. No emotion showed in his expression, but down inside he was quaking with grief.

Isaiah sat behind them. Ben saw him when he turned to look at his mother. He was glad Isaiah had come. Even though they had only known each other for a fraction of time, Isaiah had played a major part in the drama unfolding in this courtroom. He was no longer angry at the old man.

The judge continued, "And you have waived your right to legal counsel, is that correct?"

"Yes, your Honor."

"Are you ready for sentencing?" Judge Miller asked.

Ben cleared his throat and clearly stated, "No Sir. I am not!

What? It wasn't a question. It was a formality - just part of the process. You're not supposed to say no.

Judge Miller, who had been looking down at the documents on his desk, looked up, apparently taken by surprise. He slowly took a drink of water and then stared at Ben.

"Mr. Wilson, what exactly do you mean?" the judge asked.

"I would like to make a request, Your Honor!"

"Well, this is highly unusual. I cannot recall anyone appearing in my courtroom presenting a request at this particular juncture. But, I will entertain your request. What is it?"

"I would like to request the death penalty, sir."

"Yes!" came a voice from the gallery. It was Martha Fairfax. Ben didn't know them, but he had felt their presence in the courtroom. He sensed their hatred, and he didn't blame them for it. Her husband, Harvey, sat quietly, shaking his head in affirmation.

"No." came a soft whimper from Mary Wilson. "That's my baby," she cried.

"He killed my baby!" Martha screamed.

At the same time Harvey was calling out, "He deserves to die. He's a monster. Did you see what he did to my daughter? "

Fred Wilson was immediately on his feet pleading, "Two deaths don't fix things. It won't bring your daughter ba —"

"But it'll make me sleep better at night," Martha Fairfax screamed, "knowing that that monster is off the streets."

Judge Miller had been pounding his gavel demanding, "Order! I will have order in this courtroom!" He took a deep breath and let things settle down. Then he spoke in measured paces so everyone would feel his words. "I ... understand ... that you ... are very emotional ... at this ... time... However ... I will not ... I ... *will* ... *not* ... tolerate ... one ... more ... outburst!

Do you all understand?" He glared at them for a moment. "One ... more ... word ... and I will clear ... this courtroom! Do I make myself ... clear?"

Everyone sat paralyzed. It was as if time stood still. Judge Miller pushed his face forward and made a facial gesture with his eyes.

Everyone nodded.

"Now, Mr. Wilson, your crime does qualify for the death penalty, although we usually reserve that for repeat offenders. Why are you requesting the death penalty?" The judge locked his eyes on Ben and mentally faded everyone else out of focus.

"Well, ... sir, what I did ... for what I did, I deserve to die," Ben started.

Mrs. Fairfax caught herself ready to jump again when she heard her husband quietly breathe, "Amen." She settled down before it became noticeable.

Ben turned to his parents. "I'm sorry I've disappointed you." His father gazed at him with compassion in his eyes, silently communicating, "I love you, my son, no matter what you've done." There was no question about the disappointment. But neither was there any question about his father's love. His mother was weeping uncontrollably.

Ben then focused on the Fairfaxes. "What I did to your daughter, and what I have done to you is unforgiveable, and I don't expect your forgiveness. I do want you to know how sorry I am for what I took from you." The sincerity in Ben's words was wasted on them. He understood and accepted it.

Ben looked back at the judge, who was patiently allowing the drama to play out. "Your Honor, like I said ... I deserve to die. I don't want to live with the memory of what I've done. Neither do I want to live with the possibility that I might do it again. I lost control, sir. I let things build up inside of me for so long, and I lost control. What if it happens again? Can a person really change? I'm not sure I can. Please, give me the death sentence!"

The Fairfaxes were quietly chanting, "Grant it! Grant it!"

The Wilsons were quietly chanting, "Deny it! Deny it"

Isaiah just sat shaking his head.

Detective Jones, Lt. Ross, Sgt. Crowe, and Officer Simmons had varied expressions of wonder and disbelief. Not one of them was prepared to process what was taking place.

The judge's voice started rumbling from deep inside his throat and wound its way into a hum. "Mmmmmmmm ... Mr. Wilson, I'm going to have to think —"

"Uh! There's more, sir."

"What now, Mr. Wilson?" This judge was about to lose patience.

"I want to be executed by a firing squad."

There were gasps all over the room. Several members of the press jumped up to leave.

"Sit down!" Judge Miller ordered. "Officers, guard that door. Nobody leaves this courtroom."

He turned back to Ben, who was standing at the defense table. He stared at him for a long time trying to analyze his state of mind. "Mr. Wilson ... Ben ... you seem lucid. Are you playing with this court?"

"No Sir! Not at all."

"Are you trying to embarrass me or this court system?"

"Absolutely not sir. I just want justice to be served!"

"Oh, justice will be served, but in the manner I so determine. Are you trying to set this up for an insanity plea? Because I'm not go—"

"I'm not insane, your Honor."

"Well, if you are trying to create a media circus so you can get famous like all the other psychos in the past few years —"

Ben cut him short again, "Judge, a condition of my request is that there be no media present."

"Well, at least we agree on one thing. The last thing that I want is to become known as 'the hanging judge'... no, make that 'the firing squad judge' of the South Carolina lowcountry. The 'Gray man' legend is plenty enough for this county." Judge Miller was referring to the legendary 'gray ghost' who purportedly warned local residents of approaching hurricanes. It was a well-known Lowcountry legend. Many local residents and visitors hoped to catch a glimpse of the mysterious specter, though no one looked forward to the storm that followed.

Several officers started to chuckle at the judge's comment, but the judge froze them with an icy glare.

"So, young man," Judge Miller zoned in on him, "why do you want a firing squad?"

"I want to die like Francis Marion!"

"Uh! Son, if I remember my South Carolina history correctly, I'm pretty sure Francis Marion died at home at a ripe old age." Judge Miller said.

"Well, sir, I know that's what some say, but I believe he was captured and executed by a firing squad. They just keep that out of the history books to protect the legend."

Sgt. Crowe looked at Detective Jones and Lt. Ross and raised his eyebrows. Ross rolled his eyes and shook his head, as if to say, "This guy has lost it!" Jones just sagged his shoulders and looked toward Isaiah Washington. The old man had turned as pale as any black man Jones had ever seen. Isaiah sat still with a slight tremble. He didn't notice Jones' glance. The judge was rubbing his brow.

"That's how I want my execution," Ben concluded.

Judge Miller let out a long sigh for all to hear.

"Well, son. I'm going to consider your request. Bailiff, take Mr. Wilson back to his cell and stay with him. Furnish him some writing materials and get a detailed description of his request. Bring it to my chambers as soon as he's finished." Looking at Ben he added, "And son, be as detailed as you can. If I am going to consider this unusual request, I need specific details."

Ben nodded in agreement.

"Guards," Miller continued, "clear this courtroom. I'm going to my chambers for an indeterminate period of time. I want a pot of coffee and a pitcher of ice-water. And I don't want to be disturbed unless the British attack, and then somebody can bring 'Young Francis Marion' from his cell to rescue me. This court is in recess! And, members of the press, you will not release anything about this until I say so, or I will hold you in contempt. And don't give me any of that 'freedom of the press' speech. We will not turn this into a media event." With that lingering thought he disappeared through the back door leading to his private chambers. The courtroom cleared, but no one went far.

CHAPTER 22

Seated at his desk, Judge Lawrence Miller bowed his head. He placed his hands on the Bible which was a permanent fixture on his desk. Miller would often retreat to his chambers and consult the Word of God when he had difficult decisions to make on legal matters. Law was his passion, and God's law was the supreme law of all mankind, superseding every other form of law. Judge Miller considered God's infinite wisdom his greatest resource.

"Lord," he prayed, "You said in your Word, in Deuteronomy 30:19, 'This day I call heaven and earth as witnesses against you that I have set before you life and death, blessings and curses. Now choose life, so that you and your children may live.' This man that you have sovereignly brought into my courtroom - uh, *our* courtroom - has chosen death.

"Lord, I know that you direct my steps every day and that you have placed me in this office, and I know that you have brought this case before me for a divine reason that only you know. Please give me wisdom. Direct my steps and my thoughts. Lead me by your Spirit. Father, Jehoshaphat prayed, 'We do not know what to do, but our eyes are upon you.' That's what I feel right now, Lord. I don't know how to proceed in this matter, but my eyes are on you. Your thoughts are higher than my thoughts; your ways are higher than my ways, so reveal your will to me in this case. In Jesus' name I pray. Amen."

As he lifted up his eyes from prayer, his eyes fell on the calendar on his desk. It was a "Daily Guidance From The Bible" calendar that his daughter had given him. 'Verse for today' was written across the bottom. Today's verse was Joshua 1:9, "Have I not commanded you? Be strong and courageous. Do not be terrified; do not be discouraged, for the LORD your God will be with you wherever you go."

Judge Miller sighed, "Well, that's good to know, because I'd rather be anywhere than here right now facing this particular decision. But as long as you're with me, Lord, I'll be okay. Thanks for the reminder, Father."

He dialed his wife's cell phone number. He and Hannah had been married for forty years. She was his most trusted confidant and his best friend. Hannah was deeply spiritual and knowledgeable in God's Word beyond Larry's comprehension. She never ceased to amaze him with her insights and understanding of Scripture. And she was a great prayer warrior.

"Hi sweetheart," he said when she answered.

"Larry, honey I thought you were in court. How nice to hear from you."

"Yeah, your voice sure is a breath of fresh air," he smiled as he spoke. Then his expression and his voice turned serious. "Sweetheart, I've got a real dilemma here. I *am* in court. Right now, I'm in chambers, and I need your prayers and your advice. I'll tell you, sweetheart, sometimes this job is bigger than me."

"Larry," she smiled, "that job is always bigger than you."

"Yeah, baby, I know. I'm sure glad our Lord is judging mankind in the final judgment. I sure wouldn't want that job. But I've got a case today that beats all I've ever faced."

"Well, honey, I'm sure if anybody can handle it, you can ... with God's help, of course," she assured him.

"Thanks sweetheart! I appreciate your confidence in me, but wait'll you hear this one."

"Talk to me, Judge."

Theirs was a relationship truly made in heaven. Judge Miller could feel the stress loosening just talking to his lifelong companion. He and Hannah had been inseparable since they met at the University of South Carolina in Columbia forty three years ago.

Larry was from Florence, SC. He had been offered academic scholarships at several schools including Carolina and Clemson. He would have chosen Clemson, because the offer was a little more generous, but he chose Carolina because, ... well, because he was a Gamecock fan. The University of South Carolina football team had always been his favorite. That and the fact that Clemson, located in a small town in upstate South Carolina, was known as an Agricultural school, and he and his friends joked that the students drove tractors to class. None of it was true, of course, but it made the Carolina students feel more sophisticated.

Hannah was from West Virginia - a small mountain town with a name no one could quite remember. She came to USC because one of her girlfriends had chosen the school, and she felt safer venturing out into the world with a friend. She was nervous about launching out into the big, wide world after being sheltered by mountains all her life. When Larry met her, he fell for her instantly - an attractive girl with a healthy degree of modesty, small town traditions, solid values, and an iron will. He liked the combination.

Larry had experienced a life-changing conversion to Christ one year before he met Hannah. As a result, he was not interested in most of the girls at school. Actually, he wasn't interested in romantic matters at all. He was a serious student with a plan and didn't want to be sidetracked by the complications of romance. Education was his goal. But Hannah swept him off his feet. He was inextricably drawn to her. But he ran the other way. He spent hours praying, "Lord, please deliver me from these feelings. I don't have time for a relationship. Please, take this fantastic woman out of my life." A few months later, they were married.

Hannah's experience was another matter. She had become a Christian in high school. She had visited a church with her Avon lady, of all people. One day, when the Avon rep, Alice, was delivering her mother's order she invited Hannah to go to church with her on the upcoming Sunday. Being the tender-hearted person that she was, Hannah couldn't turn Alice down.

On Sunday morning, Alice drove up in an old rusty car. Hannah rushed out to the car, so Alice wouldn't have to come in after her. Secretly, she wanted to prevent Alice from getting a chance to pressure her mother and sister on religious issues. She climbed into the car, shuffled some newspapers in the floorboard with her feet to make room for her purse, and was immediately overcome with a horrendous odor. She tried not to reveal her discomfort, but apparently it was too late. Alice apologized, "Sorry about the smell. My husband delivers fish."

Oh great! What a first impression!

She was thankful they were going to a Pentecostal church. At least two fishy smelling women probably wouldn't be the strangest thing in the service that morning.

Two days later, Hannah was in the hospital for some surgery. A couple of ladies from the church visited her.

Of course! Who could forget the new girl wearing the fishy perfume!

Sandy and Brandy spent several hours with Hannah. They told her all about how God cared for her and how Jesus died for her, because, no matter how good she might be, she was still a sinner needing God's forgiveness and salvation. They prayed a beautiful prayer over her, especially Sandy. She prayed like a character out of the Bible. Hannah felt as if a wind was blowing in her heart while Sandy prayed. She wondered that it didn't register on the hospital monitor.

The ladies left Hannah with a copy of a book about a country preacher from Pennsylvania who took the gospel to gang members in New York City. Hannah read through the night. Although she could not relate to inner-city gang members, she did sense her need for God. She prayed a prayer that night, and Jesus dramatically filled her heart with a new outlook and purpose in life.

A few months later, as she was in prayer, God impressed upon Hannah to pray for her future husband. Funny! She hadn't thought about marriage. She certainly wasn't looking for a husband at this stage of her life. She bowed her head and said, "Lord, I don't understand why I'm supposed to pray for my husband, but I trust you, so, whoever he is, wherever he is, save him, protect him, prepare him ... Oh! And Lord, it wouldn't hurt if you made him good-looking, too. Amen." Hannah blushed. How silly this seemed. She could never reveal this to anyone. Yet, for some reason she felt compelled to commit to pray for this mystery man every day. So, she did!

That same week, Larry Miller was struggling with his life concept. Most of his friends were experimenting with drugs and eastern mysticism. Larry had spent the summer after graduation traveling around on his motorcycle, riding the roads and living the carefree life. But he felt an emptiness inside that none of his experiences filled. Something was missing and he couldn't put his finger on it. He was reading various books friends had given him - assorted views of life from some of the philosophers and poets of the sixties. On the one hand, it was all fascinating; on the other hand, it all just sounded like the babblings of drug induced hallucinations. Funny how what seems like an epiphany when a person is high sounds like nonsensical drivel when they're straight.

One day he picked up a book someone had given him and, in his present state of boredom and confusion, started reading just to clear his mind. It was a novel about this guy named Saul in the times of the Roman Empire. He was a religious fanatic and was trying to stamp out this new cult called Christianity, which Larry agreed was probably a good idea. But somewhere out on a desert road Saul fell off of his horse and had a vision. It was Jesus, and he told Saul that he was the Savior that the Jewish people had been waiting for and the truth that Saul had been secretly searching for. Saul's life changed from that moment. Larry wished something like that could happen to him.

The author closed the book with a recommendation to read the New Testament to find out more about this man, Saul, whose name had been changed to Paul. Larry bought a Bible and started reading. He was hungry for some kind of life change. Halfway through the Gospels Larry realized something was happening inside of him. He opened his heart and called out to God with the most ridiculous, clumsiest prayer anyone ever prayed. "God," he said, "if you're really up there, help me." God answered. The change was instantaneous.

Little did Larry know that a young lady in West Virginia had just assisted God in changing the course of his life ... and linking him to his bride-to-be.

~

"Well, babe, this one's a doozey." Miller told his wife. "I've got this case of a young man who wants me to put him in front of a firing squad."

"Oh God, help us," she prayed - her normal reaction in crisis situations. "Tell me more."

Larry hurriedly explained the whole story in a nutshell and asked his wife to intercede.

Being married to a judge, she knew she was limited in what she could reveal to the church prayer-chain, but she called her most trusted prayer partners and requested a general prayer for wisdom involving a court case. Before she disconnected with her husband, though, she said, "Honey, I just got something from the Lord. Exodus 15:13 says, 'In your unfailing love you will lead the people you have redeemed. In your strength you will guide them to your holy dwelling.' I don't know if that helps, but ..."

"It's consistent with what God just showed me from my daily verse calendar, but it still doesn't give me a clear answer - just assurance that God is with me."

"Well, I know you'll figure it out and do the right thing. And, Larry, I have a feeling of peace about this. I believe God is in it."

"Yeah, me too. Thanks, hon. Bye now. I love you."

"Love you too, babe." The receiver clicked.

The next call was to his pastor.

"Hey Larry," Pastor Olsen said, as soon as the church secretary connected the two of them. "How are you?"

"Well Jack," the judge said, "I'd be a lot better if I was on the ninth green."

"I heard that," declared the pastor. "What's on your mind?"

"I wouldn't disturb you if this wasn't urgent, Pastor —"

"Oh, I know that Judge. What can I help you with? You in court?"

"Yeah," the judge answered. "I can't really explain, you understand, but I've got the most unusual situation I've ever faced in court, and I need prayer."

"You've got it, brother," Pastor Olsen said, "But, Larry, I was expecting your call."

"You were?" the judge said, obviously surprised. "I just hung up from talking with Hannah. She couldn't have possibly —"

"No! It wasn't your wife, Larry. It was the Lord."

"What?"

"You've been on my mind for the last thirty minutes. God gave me a verse for you."

"Wow!" Judge Miller exclaimed, "He is really on top of this one, isn't He."

"He always is," the pastor assured him. "Here's the verse. Judges 6:14

'The LORD turned to him and said, 'Go in the strength you have and save Israel out of Midian's hand. Am I not sending you?' I don't know how that applies to your case, but that's what God gave me."

"Thanks, Pastor. Keep praying."

"You know I will. Let me know how things turn out."

"Oh believe me, you'll know!"

"Oh? Larry, one more thing."

"Sure! What is it?"

"Well, I just looked down at my sermon preparation for next Sunday. You won't believe what passage I have in front of me!"

"Hit me!" the judge said.

"Isaiah 30:21 'Whether you turn to the right or to the left, your ears will hear a voice behind you, saying, "This is the way; walk in it."

"Hmmm! There's something about a guy named Isaiah associated with this case. Interesting! See you Sunday, Pastor."

"Bye, Judge."

CHAPTER 23

There was a knock at the door of Judge Miller's chambers.

"Yes," he called out. "Come in!"

A petite, young clerk with long dark hair inched her way apprehensively into the office. "Please forgive me, your Honor," she spoke with a thick accent. "I know that you did not want to take a disturbance, but I was told that you have need for this document."

She handed him a legal pad. One glance told him it was the details of Ben Wilson's request. For the sake of expediency the notes had not yet been typed. Judge Miller was looking at handwritten notes taken by Officer Calvin Simmons, who had transcribed the notes as Wilson gave him the details.

"Thank you, uh ... Val..."

"Valbona," she helped him.

"Valbona, yes. Thank you, Valbona."

"It is nothing," She said as she turned and left the room. He assumed that meant "you're welcome', or maybe 'no problem'.

⌐⌐

Valbona Meta was an exchange student from Albania who had completed her freshman year at the College of Charleston and was working for the Georgetown County Court System through the summer. In a few weeks she would return to Charleston to begin her sophomore year.

Valbona was from a tiny village across the mountain from the capital city of Tirana, Albania. Having lived in the United States for just one year, Valbona still marveled at having constant electrical power and running water any time you turned on the faucet. She still laughed at how rattled her American roommates had gotten last October when a hurricane knocked out the power for two hours. In her village home of Derje, they were fortunate when they *had* power for two hours.

Valbona had fascinated her co-workers with stories of growing up in a mountain village in a third world, post-Communist country. They listened with rapt attention as she described how her father herded sheep across the mountains - how he would shear the sheep and her mother would spin the wool and make clothes, socks, and blankets for the family. She described how her parents would beat out the wheat in front of their small home. Her mother cooked on a stove fueled by firewood. Her father and brother would eat first. Then, when they finished, she and her mother would eat.

"What if your father and brother didn't leave enough food for you and your mother?" someone asked.

"Not to worry," Valbona assured them. "Mother and I ate plenty while we were cooking."

As the laughter died down someone asked, "Did your father know?"

"If he did," she answered, "he never spoke of it."

They laughed again.

Valbona described the fabulous trips to Tirana, the capital city. After a two hour hike down the mountain trail, they would flag down a *furgon* (a passenger van) and pay twenty *leke* (about fifteen cents) for a ride into the city to buy family supplies at the *pazari* (the outdoor market).

The girls of the village were only provided a basic primary education, while the boys were given more academic opportunities, but had to earn the right to progress in education. Few made it to college. Valbona's parents sent her to live with an uncle in Tirana so that she could continue in school. She finished high school and qualified for university. Then she won a place in the exchange program and was now studying in the United States. She hoped to get a degree in International Business and return to Albania to help move her country forward.

Valbona was asked at one point, "How did it feel to grow up in such extreme poverty?"

"Ha!" Valbona laughed. "We did not think of it as poverty. It was just life. It was the way we lived. We had what we needed in order to live. That is all we expected. In fact, our leaders told us that the Americans were going to attack us to steal our wealth." A stunned hush went through the room.

"Are you serious?" a voice exclaimed.

"Oh, yes! Our people took it very seriously!" Valbona attested. "Our mountainsides are dotted with more than eighty thousand concrete bunkers built to protect us from your attack."

"But, why would they believe that?" someone asked.

"Well, for one thing, we did not know any Americans. For another thing, the Albanian people were not allowed to question government leaders. My country was completely closed off from the rest of the world until 1991."

Valbona could not believe how naive these Americans were. She held no resentment about it though. She realized that, in many ways, these people were just as much in the dark about what was going on in the rest of the world as her people had been.

CHAPTER 24

"**M**r. Wilson," Judge Miller began after everyone had been gathered back into the courtroom, "after much arduous deliberation, and to be perfectly candid, much prayer and counsel, for reasons that I still don't fully understand, I am granting your request to die by execution before a firing squad.

"The details of your request are acceptable to this court - five marksmen at ten paces, at first light, no media, a select group of witnesses including the officers involved in your arrest, your family and the family of the victim, members of this court, and your friend, Isaiah Washington," the judge read off the list. "And you want to be executed here in Georgetown. Why is that?"

"Well, sir," Ben explained, "I started my life in Georgetown. I'd might as well end it here."

"Well, normally executions would be performed in Columbia, but there hasn't been much normal about this case anyway, so we'll allow it. One curious question though," the judge continued. "Why the specification about one gun containing a blank?"

"For the protection of the marksmen, your Honor," Ben said.

"I'm not sure I understand," the judge cocked his head to one side.

"It leaves each shooter with a reasonable doubt as to whether he fired the fatal shot. Each marksman can comfort himself with the possibility that his gun was the one with the blank and had no effect whatsoever on the outcome of the execution. Therefore, no feeling of responsibility for taking a life," Ben explained.

"Hmm! Very interesting! And this was your idea?" the judge asked.

"No sir!" Ben said. "It's actually standard procedure with firing squads."

"Well, I don't have any experience with firing squads, so this is a first for me." The judge cleared his throat. "Benjamin Wilson, you are scheduled to face the firing squad one week from today. May God have mercy on your soul. This court session is adjourned!" With a crack of his gavel the business was ended.

⌢

Ben was placed in a cell away from the other prisoners. He had his own personal death row of sorts there in the Georgetown County Jailhouse. He was glad he didn't have spend his last week in the cell with Jerry, but then again, it sure did get lonely.

Time passed like a rowboat in quicksand. There was little to do for a man confined in an eight-by-eight cell. There was a TV across the room outside of his cell, but what was the point? There were books, games, puzzles, but what could be interesting or entertaining when you have an appointment with death? He thought a lot, but thought is depressing when it's leading nowhere.

There were several preachers who came by wanting to talk the 'dead man walking' into getting 'saved'. *Strange,* Ben thought, *how the religionists come out of the woodwork to help a man prepare to die. Why don't they try harder to prepare a man to live? Well, maybe they tried, and I just wasn't listening.*

Ben thought about something else. Some of the things that Isaiah said to him, he had heard before, back in Sunday School when he was a young boy. But those teachers didn't sound nearly as passionate or convincing as Isaiah. Neither did most of these death row preachers. *I guess they figure a dying man is an easy convert,* he thought. It seemed that most of the people he had heard talk about God talked about him like it was a duty ... like they had to meet a quota ... like God and Jesus were products they were selling.

Isaiah talked about God like he was a friend that he wanted me to meet, not like a product he wanted me to buy.

Isaiah seemed to have a whole different perspective on this religion thing. But the old man was real big on the idea that Jesus died for people. He said that Jesus actually took our place - took the punishment we deserved. Well, maybe he died for those good people - like Isaiah, and maybe Judge Miller, a-n-d maybe Detective Jones ... and maybe even Ben's mother. But trade his life for Ben's? Nah! Not a chance. That life was already too far gone. No chance of salvaging that one.

"Yeah, right!" Ben muttered to himself, "Like Jesus is going to take my place in front of this firing squad. Get real! Whatever you want to believe old man. But this is real life. Jesus is long gone."

CHAPTER 25

The week passed. The day of reckoning had dawned. Ben was led, handcuffed, to the jail yard. In the center of the yard was a post, specially put there in response to his request. They propped him against the post, but he asked that he not be tied to it. He wanted to face this like a man. The guards looked to their commander. He nodded, and they backed away leaving Ben to stand free.

Roughly twenty yards from the post stood a squad of five guards with rifles. Some of the men had to be forced to accept this duty; others were eager to make history, and so they volunteered. One of the guards that led Ben out started to put a blindfold on him. Ben refused. *Francis Marion wouldn't have worn a blindfold. He would face his accusers – his executioners – face to face – eyeball to eyeball.*

The moments seemed to pass ever so slowly – minutes felt like hours – seconds felt like minutes.

He scanned the group of witnesses. The jail guards were there, as well as the officers who had assisted in apprehending him - Crowe, Marsh, and the others. Detective Jones was there. And Officer Simmons, too. There was a priest - he could tell by the clerical collar. Beside him was another man in a suit who looked familiar - probably one of the preachers who had tried to 'save his soul' on death row. His dad was there. His mother was not. She couldn't bear to witness the execution of her only son. The

Fairfaxes, Liz's parents, were there in the back. They wanted to see him die, but they didn't want him to see them.

Isaiah was not there. *Can't blame him*, Ben thought. Isaiah had visited him during the week and tried to talk him out of this. He told Ben that he didn't agree with the death penalty, because "a man can change in time" he had said. "A man might come to hisself and repent."

Ben had heard people say that, in the moments before death, a man's life passes before his eyes. He had always thought that was just a fabrication to glorify the moment of death. Now it was becoming a reality for him. Pictures – no, videos – of his life began to play in his mind. He could see himself playing at the beach, learning to drive, graduating from high school. It all seemed to flash before him. He didn't know where the memories were coming from. He wasn't conjuring them up. They came at random.

Then there was a drum-roll – Ben had insisted on a drum-roll.

"Ready!" came the call. He could hear the rifles being lifted. A rush of fear engulfed him.

Ben's mind drifted to a time when he was five or six years old. He and his mother and sister were at home on South Island Road. His dad was at work. A severe hurricane had blown in from the Atlantic rather quickly and his dad was not able to drive home from work because of the gale force winds. The sky was black. The rain pelted against the house. The wind howled through every crack in the wood framed structure. He was afraid. His younger sister was crying. They could hear things crashing against the sides of the house. His mother led them to the small hallway in the very center of the house where there were several doorways. This would be the strongest and safest part of the construction. They sat on the floor, and his mother held them and told them stories until the storm passed. It never occurred to him until now that his mom was probably as afraid as they were, but she never showed it. How he wished she could hold him now.

The scene changed. He and his dad were in the garage working on ... well, he couldn't remember what ... when they heard a blood curdling scream. The sound of it seemed unending. He could tell it was his little sister's voice. He followed his dad, in a dead run, to the corner of the house. There was his sister in the middle of the back yard. Two feet in front of her was a coiled rattlesnake, mouth wide open, fangs extended and poised to strike. His dad ran into the garage and grabbed a garden hoe. He rushed to the snake and chopped it in half before it could strike his sister. He had never seen anyone so brave – not even on TV. He stood here now realizing that he had never told his dad how proud he was of his death-defying act. Now he would never have the chance.

His memories continued to flood in like waves on the coastline, one after another. Each memory seemed to have a will of its own.

He thought of his high school days. The girls would scowl at him. The boys would tease him and pick on him. He was often the brunt of jokes. It was a painful memory. This was where it all started – the teasing, the ridiculing, the humiliation. The memory crushed in on him like a tidal wave. They called him 'loser'. They called him 'reject'. They treated him like a leper. He had always been treated this way. No wonder he had become so twisted. No wonder ...

Then a thought occurred to Ben. Why had he never wondered *why* they made fun of him? Here, in the last moments of his life, Ben Wilson found himself pondering the deeper issues of human behavior. What is it that makes people find it necessary to degrade other people? Why do people seem to revel in someone else's pain? Could it be that *they* were the ones with the problem? ... that they were the ones in pain? Picking on him made them feel better about themselves? Was it really so important for them to be 'on top' that they found it necessary to put him and others 'on the bottom'? What was their problem?

Yeah! That's it! It was *their* problem - not *his*. All of his life he had allowed other people's opinions about him to determine his opinion about himself. What a waste! How wrong he had been. That's why he stood here today before this firing squad.

"Aim!" He heard the guns cock. In a matter of seconds his life would end.

His mind refocused - changed channels. He was in the apartment with Liz. The details that his mind had previously blocked now came into focus. He was back in that room - in that moment. He could see the invitation in her eyes - could feel the hotness of her breath, the smoothness of her skin, and then ... the sting of her humiliation. He heard her screaming obscenities at him ... laughing at him ... that wicked laugh ringing, echoing to the very core of his being. He saw her mouth like a deep, black pit sucking him in ... devouring him ...severing from him any thread of dignity he had left. He felt the rage engulfing him ... taking control. He saw himself pick up the elephant bookend. He smashed it into her face. And then she was silent. She lay on the floor in front of him ... blood gushing from what used to be her face.

"Oh God, What have I done?" He wasn't sure if he had thought these words or actually said them out loud.

"Fire!" There it was! He waited to feel the piercing of bullets in the next split second. He heard the shots. Ba-bam! Bam! Bam! He saw puffs of smoke emitting from each gun. He could hear the bullets grinding down the gun barrels on the way to his waiting body. He could almost visualize the exit of the charges, the vibration of the wind as the projectiles left the gun barrels and pierced the air. He anticipated the feel of the piercing bullets in the next split second.

There was a blur ... movement. What was happening? He didn't feel anything. Was he dead? He didn't think so. But then, how does a person know when he's dead?

There was a gasp. Several gasps. There was a buzz of commotion. Ben tried to focus - to figure out what was happening. Then his vision cleared, and the reality slapped him like a sheet of ice. He let out a blood-curdling scream, "NO!" His voice echoed, it seemed, through eternity.

Ben looked down. There, at his feet ... lay Isaiah ... bleeding ... choking on his own blood. At the command to fire, Isaiah had leapt out of the shadows in time to intercept the bullets.

"No! No! Noooo!" Ben cried, "Isaiah! What have you done? Why ...?"

"I took your place ... jes' ..." he gurgled on the blood in his throat, "jes' ... like ... Jesus did," he struggled the words out.

"No! You can't ..." Ben tried to protest.

"Already ... did," Isaiah coughed.

"Ben," Isaiah motioned for Ben to lean closer. He coughed a couple of times and whispered, "Surrender!"

"What? What do you mean surrender? They caught me! I'm in custody. I was supposed to be executed," Ben screamed through tears.

"Not ... to them." Isaiah coughed and gurgled on more blood. He pointed upward. "To ... Him."

Tears were streaming down Ben's face. He shook his head to clear his vision. His hands were still bound behind his back. He sniffed. His nose was running from the crying.

Officers were clearing the scene - ushering the visitors out of the area. They had to maintain order - had to prevent anything else from happening in the confusion of this execution gone wrong. Two guards were attempting to lift Ben to his feet. He resisted. Detective Jones signaled them to leave him alone - let him talk to the old man. EMS workers were making their way to the wounded man, but Jones already knew his wounds were fatal. There was no rush.

Judge Miller moved closer to the scene.

"Isaiah, what have you done? Why?..." Ben sobbed.

"Ben, I ... already 'splained it ... to ya. A man ... can change." Isaiah took a few more labored breaths and struggled to speak. Time was running out. He had to make Ben understand. "Ben ... I done took ... your place ... in ... this here ... execution. Now ... you take ... my ... place."

"Take your place?" Ben questioned. "How?"

"Sur ... render." It was the last word Isaiah ever spoke.

Ben threw himself on the man's body and sobbed like a baby. Several guards had to drag him away.

CHAPTER 26

Hours later, Ben sat, unshackled, in an interview room at the jailhouse. Detective Jones and Judge Miller sat across the table. Ben was still shuddering from his sobbing episode. He was emotionally drained and physically exhausted from the heaving. He had continued to weep for two hours after the attempted execution. The two men across the table wore somber expressions.

"What happens now?" he asked, not to either man in particular.

"Well," Jones spoke. He glanced at the judge for help. None was offered. "As far as I understand it, we carried out an execution here today, and ..." a long pause, "... it's over."

"What do you mean, it's over?"

Judge Miller spoke up, "Mr. Wilson, what he means is that you have been given a second chance."

"You mean I can just go?" Ben said, not really believing what he had just heard. "You mean I'm free?"

"Well, yes ... and no!" said the judge.

"What ... what does that mean?"

The judge spoke again, "Mr. Wilson, as far as we are concerned, we have fulfilled our legal obligations. I don't think we can execute a man twice for the same crime. I would assume the rule of 'double jeopardy' applies here."

What's the rule of double jeopardy?" Ben asked.

"Never mind. Suffice it to say that, as much as it pains me to release a murderer who has not paid his debt to society, it appears that your debt has been paid by someone else. In the strictest sense, fair or not, justice has been served.

"But," and the judge spoke very firmly and deliberately, "you still owe a debt to the one who sacrificed his life to save yours. I heard Mr. Washington's last words to you. He said, 'I took your place in this execution. Now you take my place.' Ben Wilson, it was a mighty big man who traded his life for yours. It seems to me that you have some mighty big shoes to fill."

Detective Jones spoke up, "Ben, I can't pretend to understand why Isaiah Washington would trade his life for yours. I don't see how you have much of a future unless you make some pretty big changes. So, I'm telling you, you'd better be worth what Washington gave up for you. And Ben," he concluded with a threatening look, "I'll be watching you!"

Two weeks later, Officer Cal Simmons ran into Detective George Jones at the Georgetown County Courthouse.

"Hey Cal, what brings you down to Georgetown," Jones asked.

"Oh, just testifying in a routine court case. Nothing quite as exciting as the Wilson case. By the way, whatever happened to Wilson?"

"Isaiah Washington made arrangements before his death with a local attorney. He legally transferred ownership of his cabin to Wilson. Three days after Washington's death, the attorney served the papers to Ben. Next day, Ben packed up and hiked out to the cabin. He's been out there ever since," Jones told him.

"Has anybody talked to him?"

"No, but we're keeping tabs on him. I'll tell you, it'll be a miracle if that boy survives out there in the swamps."

"Yeah, he'll probably get eaten by gators. It would serve him right. I can't believe how he got out of this thing."

"Well, I don't know Cal. Isaiah Washington apparently thought this kid was worth it. We'll see."

EPILOGUE:

Ben is now a free man. Or is he? Can a man start over after such a traumatic experience? Can a man ever hope to live any semblance of a normal life after such a crushing disaster?

Will he stay at the cabin Isaiah left for him? Can he survive the hazardous conditions of the swamplands any more than he could survive the wrath of society?

Isaiah said, "now you take my place." Does that mean that Ben is to confine himself to the life a hermit, shunning society that fears and rejects him?

What should have been the end for Ben Wilson was only the beginning.

A NOTE FROM THE AUTHOR:

In 1973, I received Jesus as my Savior and my Lord. Everything changed. Music had been my life. But then I discovered that true life is found in Jesus. (John 14:6 Jesus said to him, "I am the way, and the truth, and the life; no one comes to the Father, but through Me.") I threw out five years worth of songwriting and started fresh with new reason to sing and a new song in my heart. Later that year I wrote a song called "Firing Squad", which I later recorded. In 2009, I decided to turn the song into a story. At the time I didn't imagine I would every publish it. It was just fun to write. (Believe it or not I wrote the whole book on my Blackberry.) Here I am, nearly four years later, going to print.

Some of the stories in the book are actually biographical. It was me that fell off the boat trailer and my cousin and a friend laughed. (I guess I did look pretty funny.) My dad did kill the rattlesnake threatening my sister. The salvation and marriage of the judge and his wife is pretty close to Patti's and my story. I grew up in the South Carolina lowcountry and lived in Albania for a few years.

I hope you enjoy reading this as much as I enjoyed writing it.

Rick Roberts

(Watch for the sequel "The Transformation of Ben Wilson".
Check our website for updates. www.prroberts.com)

Previous publications:
"New Life from Disaster", Pentecostal Evangel, July 24, 1994 (Official Magazine of the Assemblies of God.)
"Just in Time", Pentecostal Evangel, August 28, 1994
"Kjo Eshte Jeta" (This is the Life), printed in Albania, 2001

Recordings:
"Live In His Presence", 1981, cassette tape with 10 original songs
"Cancelled Debt", 1990, CD and cassette with 12 original songs
"Revive Us", 1995, original song recorded by GPH Music, Music Ministry Network